John Dennis

The realms of gold

A book for youthful students of English literature

John Dennis

The realms of gold
A book for youthful students of English literature

ISBN/EAN: 9783337203047

Printed in Europe, USA, Canada, Australia, Japan

Cover: Foto ©Andreas Hilbeck / pixelio.de

More available books at **www.hansebooks.com**

THE
REALMS OF GOLD

A BOOK FOR YOUTHFUL STUDENTS
OF ENGLISH LITERATURE

BY

JOHN DENNIS

London
GRANT RICHARDS
1899

PREFACE

THERE is a definite purpose in this little volume, and I hope that it will be in some measure accomplished. My aim is to create in youthful readers a love of good literature, and in the early days of life that love can be most readily awakened by appealing to the poets and to the imaginative writers, whose works, akin to poetry, not only give delight to the young but are among their best teachers.

If once a love be felt for the things that are noble in our literature, if but a glimpse be gained of the Realms whose riches are free to all who have learnt to find in them a home, the pursuit of knowledge instead of being a drudgery will give a new impulse

A

and animation to life. Should these "Talks" prove of service in the promotion of so good an end, they will not have been written in vain. The "Realms of Gold" was suggested by several papers in *Good Words*, of which some use has been made with the kind permission of the proprietors, but by far the larger portion of the book is printed for the first time.

J. D.

WONSTON,
CROWBOROUGH.

CONTENTS

SUMMARY OF CONTENTS

FIRST TALK

SECOND TALK

6   The Realms of Gold

Milton (1608-1674)—His self-dedication to Poetry—His youthful Genius and later Works—John Bunyan (1628-1688), *Pilgrim's Progress*—Jeremy Taylor (1613-1667), *Rules of Holy Living and Dying*—Quotations from Taylor and Bunyan—Quotations from George Herbert (1593-1632) —Herbert compared with Henry Vaughan (1621-1695)— Milton the supreme Poet of the Age—Greater popularity of John Dryden (1631-1700)—Fame of Abraham Cowley (1618-1667)—Quotation from Edmund Waller (1605-1687).

THIRD TALK

The Eighteenth Century—Its Characteristics—Daniel Defoe (1661-1731)—His *Robinson Crusoe*—His versatile Life— The Essayists—Joseph Addison (1672-1719)—His Charm as a Humourist—*Sir Roger de Coverley*—Macaulay on Addison —Sir Richard Steele (1672-1729), the Originator of the popular Essay, and Friend of Addison—His Faults and Virtues—Oliver Goldsmith (1728-1774), one of the best-beloved of Poets—His strange Career—*The Vicar of Wakefield, The Citizen of the World*, Quotations from—Thomas Gray (1716-1771)—His odd Fancy about the *Elegy*—His attractive Character—Love of Mountain Scenery—Travels in the English Lake District and in the Highlands of Scotland—Such delight in Nature incomprehensible to the Queen Anne Wits—Mountain-climbing a Growth of the Century and partly stimulated by Byron and Wordsworth— Mr. Ruskin on the "Pathetic Fallacy": an Illustration from his own Writings—William Cowper (1731-1800) compared with James Thomson (1700-1748) and with Wordsworth— His Gifts as a Letter-Writer—Scottish Poetry—Jean Adams (——1765)—Isabel Pagan (1740-1821)—Jane Elliot (1727-1805)—Alison Cockburn (——1794)—Lady Grisell Baillie (1665-1746)—Lady Nairne (1766-1845)—Lady Anne Lindsay (1750-1825)—Robert Burns (1759-1796)—Dr. Johnson (1709-1784)—His unique Position—His Writings and his Talk—Boswell's *Life*—Its inexhaustible Interest— Mr. Arnold on Johnson's *Lives of the Poets*—Macaulay's false Estimate of Boswell.

FOURTH TALK

An Answer to the Question, "What is the Use of Poetry?"—
Coleridge's Estimate of Poetry, and Wordsworth's—Popu-
larity no Test of Merit—Samuel Rogers (1763-1855)—His
Pleasures of Memory—Byron's Estimate of contemporary
Poets—Coleridge and Keats at one time ridiculed, and
Wordsworth most unpopular—George Crabbe (1754-1832)
—Admired by Scott and Charles Fox, by Cardinal Newman
and Mr. Swinburne—Tennyson's Estimate of his Poetry—
His peculiar Merits—Quotations from his Poems—William
Wordsworth (1770-1850)—His Place in the Front Rank
of our Poets—His Deficiencies partly owing to a lack of
Humour—In this respect contrasted with Cowper—Lord
Selborne's Estimate of him as a Teacher—His Theory of
Poetry—The artificial Diction of the previous Century
described — His Patriotism — His Sense of Joy — This
Characteristic notable also in his Friend, Samuel Taylor
Coleridge (1772-1834) — Illustrative Quotations — Char-
acteristics of Coleridge's Poetry—Hartley Coleridge (1796-
1849)—His Verse quoted—Robert Southey (1774-1843)—
Lives chiefly by his Prose Writings—His Character—John
Keats (1795-1821)—One of the most Poetical of Poets—
His *Ode to Autumn* and Sonnet on *Chapman's Homer*
quoted—His brief Life and great Sorrows—Percy Bysshe
Shelley (1792-1822)—His Genius as a Lyric Poet—One of
the Saddest of Poets—His Invocation to the *Spirit of
Delight*—Lord Byron (1788-1824)—His great temporary
Popularity—Reasons why he is less regarded now—Elizabeth
Barrett Browning (1801-1861)—Her unquestionable Genius
but defective Taste—Her finest Verse due to Personal
Feeling—Difference between a Poet and a Poetaster—
Thomas Hood (1799-1845)—A Minor Poet but a true
one—Fettered by Circumstances—His serious Poems, and
their influence.

FIFTH TALK

Sir Walter Scott—His Claims on youthful Readers—Compared
in some respects with Shakespeare—His poetical Genius

8   The Realms of Gold

depreciated by some Critics, and for what Reasons—His
Forte that of a Ballad-Writer—His Passion for Nature and
for Song—*The Lay of the Last Minstrel*—Quotation from
Marmion—Influence of *The Lady of the Lake*—Scott's
Lyrics—*The Waverley Novels*—The most striking Features
of the Novelist's Genius—Quotations—Scott's Prose Style
—His broad View of Life—His Deficiencies—The Estimate
formed of him by Men of Intellect and Genius.

SIXTH TALK

Alfred Lord Tennyson (1809-1892)—The most gifted Poet since
Wordsworth—His happy Life compared with that of Spenser
—His Devotion to his Art—His Lyrical Genius—Quota-
tions—Characteristics of his Poetry—Its Music—Its de-
scriptive Power—Its Variety and Perfection of Style—
Bishop Butler's Estimate of the Imagination—Concluding
Remarks.

THE REALMS OF GOLD

FIRST TALK

I REMEMBER when a boy that my first feeling upon being left to browse at will in a large library was one of bewilderment and irresolution. The wealth around me was so abundant that I did not know what to appropriate. There was the sense of greatness on the one side and of incapacity on the other. Book after book was taken down from the shelves, glanced at, and returned unread. Thousands of volumes were around me, and yet, dearly though I loved books, I felt disappointed, and could not understand the feeling. My own little library of fifty or sixty volumes had been a source to me of unbounded pleasure, and here in a Realm of Gold I felt much as a hungry man may feel who gazes upon a feast to which he must not sit down.

I did not know at first what ailed me, and it was long before I discovered that in literature as in life what Wordsworth calls "unchartered freedom" is good neither for mind nor body. The largest intellect can only expand healthily within well-defined limits, and for most of us whose intellects are not large, it is necessary that in reading as well as in other employments we should have a distinct purpose. Sir Walter Scott has described the delight he felt as a schoolboy when, having scraped a few shillings together, he was able to buy a copy of Percy's *Reliques of Ancient English Poetry*, and how, sitting under a huge platanus tree, he forgot, notwithstanding the sharp appetite of thirteen, the hour of dinner while feasting on these famous ballads. It is not every young reader whose taste for a special subject is as distinctly marked as Walter Scott's; but I have mentioned this anecdote to show how necessary it is to have a bent in some direction in order to make a good use of books. Had Scott in his schoolboy days been turned loose in a library such as he afterwards formed at Abbotsford he would have found the food he wanted.

There is a time in the lives of many young people when the ideal world of books is more to them than the world of living men and women, and it is well that they should enjoy this delicious world while they can. The sorrows of life, its anxieties, its sufferings, its regrets, come soon enough to all of us! Live then for a while in the joyous land of books through the happy spring hours, when May-blossoms scent the air and the songs of the lark and thrush make the heart leap with pleasure! Let the poets sing for you their choicest songs, and the genius of the novelist bear you as upon wings into a fair region of romance; but be firm and brave enough never so to yield to the enchantment of books as to become their slave. Reading may be one of the wisest pursuits in life; it may also be one of the idlest, and I scarcely know any occupation more enervating to the mind than the aimless, shiftless habit of taking up a book in order to make the time pass, and of glancing from topic to topic in the magazines for the amusement of the hour. I say the *habit*, because there are doubtless times when reading for mere amusement can be as readily justified as playing at cricket or lawn-tennis. The perusal of a good novel may prove more than an amusement, and is a wholesome recreation, but to devour fiction indiscriminately to the neglect of more solid studies is to squander the season of life, which of all seasons is the most precious. People forget or do not know that the mind may be as much wasted in reading as in sheer idleness if books are read without judgment, without selection, and with the careless mind that accepts an opinion as a truth or is indifferent whether it be a truth or not.

I may be wrong, but it seems to me that a want of earnestness and reverence is one of the signs of the day. Indifference is the death of the intellect and the heart. There are people who have no strong interest in anything. They are wanting in ambition, in energy, in every purpose which gives a zest and nobility to life. Wherever there is manifested a glow of enthusiasm, an ardour of aspiration, these dead-alive people treat it with contempt. Wanting vitality themselves, they endeavour to quench its spark in others. Keep as clear of such acquaintances as you can. There is nothing to be gained and much that you will be in danger of losing in their company. It is not, of course, essential that men or women should love books, but it is essential to all worthy living that they should keep before them some goal which it demands an effort to reach, some object to which they can dedicate their energies and yield their love. These Talks are to be about books and authors, but I should be leading you widely astray if I made you think that there are not spheres of thought and occupation affording as wide a scope as literature, in some cases even wider, for the exercise of intellect and heart.

Remember always that literature is not life; you have to live your own lives, to think your own thoughts, and to act in many cases on a responsibility which is distinctly personal. Nothing that has been done or said will avail you much in times of difficulty or temptation unless it has strengthened character and given freedom to the judgment. With great truth does Cowper say :—

> Knowledge and wisdom far from being one
> Have ofttimes no connection. Knowledge dwells
> In heads replete with thoughts of other men,
> Wisdom in minds attentive to their own.
> Knowledge, a rude unprofitable mass,
> The mere materials with which wisdom builds,
> Till smoothed and squared and fitted to its place
> Does but encumber whom it seems to enrich.

And Shakespeare with his wonderful sagacity shows his contempt for plodders who have gained nothing save "base authority from others' books."

In his diary Crabb Robinson writes :— "Wordsworth spoke of Southey with great feeling and affection. He said it is painful to see how completely dead Southey is become to all but books. He is amiable and obliging, but when he gets away from his books he seems restless and as if out of his element." And a letter written by Southey in his old age corroborates the impression formed by Wordsworth. "Books are all but everything to me," he writes. " I live with them and by them, and might almost say for them and in them." Southey, one of the best of men, was a most affectionate husband and father. The passion which led him to accumulate fifteen thousand volumes never lessened his love of wife, of children, or of home. But it was a failing which grew upon him with the years, and no doubt Wordsworth was right in choosing rather to lose his interest in books than in men, if it were necessary to decide between them. He would not have found the choice difficult, for Wordsworth never had a loyal regard for books, and would, it has been said, open a valuable volume with a greasy knife.

"Thousands of volumes," De Quincey writes, "that have given rapturous delight to millions of ingenuous minds, for Wordsworth were absolutely a dead letter, closed and sealed up from his sensibilities and his powers of appreciation, not less than colours from a blind man's eye." The enthusiasm for literature felt so strongly by men like Dr. Johnson and Southey was unknown to Wordsworth, but Johnson, unlike Southey, found even more enjoyment in the clash of mind with mind in society. Scott, too, was a great reader, but he was also using the term in its best sense—"a man of the world" —and read in order to live and work among his fellows, instead of living to read.

This is the spirit I would urge you to cultivate with regard to books. Love them as warmly as you will, but endeavour also to love them wisely. And avoid singularity in your attachment. There is a foolish fashion in the book world which youthful readers are apt to follow. They are prone to admire works because they are rare, and to praise authors because they are unknown. But in almost every instance the forgotten book is a worthless book, and if it be revived to live a brief life in a modern dress, the strongest feeling it excites is curiosity. The literary trifler may make much of the toy he has discovered, but the lover of what is sound in literature will not waste his time upon playthings when so much that is beautiful and noble claims his attention. In your studies, as in your conduct in life, the old paths will always be found the safest and the best. Walk in them until they grow familiar, and then you will be able to judge for yourselves how far it may be well to stray in search of what is new and strange.

If you have the instinct for books that makes the very sight of them a delight, you will begin, I hope, quite early in life to form a library of your own. No matter how small your supply of money, some of it should be spent on books, so that you may have these choice friends near at hand to yield at any moment the delight for which you crave. The authors that feed the circulating libraries may supply you perhaps with recreation in leisure hours, but the volumes that will influence character and give scope and energy to the mind must not be fitful visitors, but daily companions.

Many a work has been written telling the student how to read books, and to guide him in the choice of them. Such advice may be of good service at the outset, and yet it can be but of partial benefit. There is as much variety in minds as in nature, and what may prove of service in one case may be an obstacle to progress in another. What is your purpose in reading ? I suppose you will answer that you read partly to acquire knowledge and partly for the sake of enjoyment. Two reasonable objects doubtless, if indeed they are not one, since to gain knowledge is itself a pleasure of the highest order. And yet there are two purposes, for which study should be pursued, and two classes of books which minister to those purposes. The one class we read for facts, the other class for ideas, although it is almost needless to say that some volumes, "the precious life-blood of master spirits," combine both.

To the student a strong foundation of facts is indispensable, and the Realms of Gold can be best approached through the gate of history. Fully to understand, for example, the allusions of a Shakespeare or a Milton demands a large amount of preparatory knowledge : and since every author is in a measure the product of his age, and Butler could not have written

Hudibras nor Pope *The Dunciad* in our century, it follows that the more we know of the age in which a famous writer lived the better shall we appreciate his genius. The record of the historian is illuminated by the fire of the poet; the novelist interprets the sober pages of the chronicler. So closely is the literature of a nation linked to its history that the student will be a loser if he attempts to divide them. And this holds good with regard to imaginative literature quite as much as to the branches which pedagogues consider more solid.

Literature at its highest level consists of the wisest and most beautiful thoughts expressed in the best words. Every great people has produced a noble literature, and this is indeed one of the chief signs of its greatness.

We have the literature of the Jews in the books which form our Bible; Greece produced a literature unequalled to this day for perfection of language; Rome that once ruled the world, did so first by the sword, then by her laws, and then by the poets, rhetoricians, and historians who have made the Latin language so famous. The most civilised of modern nations, too, can each boast a great national literature, but not one

of these has, on the whole, a literature equal
to that which is open to English readers.
Here, there is a vast storehouse full to
overflowing of precious treasures, and the
wealth piled up may so puzzle the youth
who looks in at the door that he will
perhaps hesitate to enter. What can he
do? he may ask; how can he best use the
gifts which wise and great Englishmen
have left for his service? I will endeavour
to answer this question. You know the
difference between land in its natural state
and land that has been drained and manured,
that has felt the ploughshare and the
harrow; you know also the difference
between the flowers of our lanes and fields
and the flowers which grow in a well-cared-
for garden. A similar difference may be
seen between men whose minds have been
allowed to run wild and men whose minds
have been carefully cultivated. The com-
parison, however, is in one respect an unfair
one, because nature, however untended, is
always beautiful; but there is no beauty in
a mind which like the garden of the
sluggard contains nothing but wild briars,
thistles, and weeds.

In order, then, to read books so as to get
good out of them the mind needs culture,

which is not mere knowledge, although that is indispensable, but the *power* of seeing what is beautiful and true in literature and of detecting what is feeble and false. This power cannot be acquired off-hand like a lesson. Many readers never do gain it. They read without discrimination, they have no ear for the beauty of words, no sensitive perception of what is noble in thought. They understand the necessity of making a statement accurately, but cannot see that it is of the slightest consequence in what form the thing is said. To them a police report or a summary of news is as much literature as the essays of Addison or of Charles Lamb, and their approval or contempt of a book is alike worthless.

The only method of acquiring a just knowledge of literature is to study the great masters.

A knowledge of the classics of Greece and Rome is perhaps the soundest foundation upon which to build up an acquaintance with the more varied and in some respects wealthier literature of modern times. "Read the Ancients first," said Wordsworth, "and then come to us." Yes! but it is very possible, as we know by a vast number of examples, to be familiar with the classics of

Greece and Rome without any perception or enjoyment of their worth as literature.

Do not, therefore, be discouraged if you have not this advantage. The study of our own authors, and especially of the English poets, whose wealth is exhaustless, will yield all that is needed for the cultivation of a literary taste. The authorised version of the English Bible has infinitely higher claims upon your study than are due to its literary merits, but as a model of composition it is unrivalled. There is no prose in the language more harmonious than this incomparable translation, none that is at once so vigorous, so simple, and so idiomatic. It would seem impossible that any reader familiar with its dignity of style can fail to distinguish between majesty of thought and grandiloquence, between impassioned utterance and tawdry rhetoric, between the rhythmical flow of sentences which fall on the ear like music, and the flowery and verbose style, by the help of which many a modern writer endeavours to conceal poverty of thought. And would it be possible after listening to the enchanting music of Spenser or to the majestic utterances of Milton, the "God-gifted, organ-voice of England," to prefer the thinner notes of versemen whose pretty knack of rhyming enables them to snatch a temporary fame? There is an atmosphere in literature, as well as in life, and in it we breathe diviner air and gain freedom and joy.

A significant test of a book's merit is that it will bear reading again and again. We turn to the great works of genius, not so much for information as for suggestion and delight. They strengthen us intellectually, they raise us spiritually, they give a fuller sense of life, they make life more harmonious. It may be sometimes difficult to say what we have learnt from a great poet or imaginative prose writer, but we are conscious that his words have invigorated us. Much is demanded from an author who aspires to write a work that may claim to rank as literature. His book must be pure in style, rich in thought, strong with the vital power that breathes life into his readers, great in conception, beautiful in form, with enough of imagination to give it harmony and enough of enthusiasm to kindle it in others while maintaining the sweet reasonableness that keeps passion within bounds.

This is doubtless a high standard, and

perhaps not wholly attainable, but it is one which an author who respects his calling will aim at, and one, I think, that you should keep before you in judging of the books you read.

The story of the century now so near its close has been the most spirit-stirring in our history. Not even the great age of Elizabeth can boast of deeds so noble and generous, of courage more heroic, of a spirit more adventurous. And the physical courage and love of enterprise that marked the earlier period, while as prominent as ever in Englishmen, has been tempered by virtues unknown or nearly so to all save a select few of our Elizabethan forefathers. Our country from the days of Nelson and Wellington to the days in which we can boast of such heroes as Lord Roberts and Lord Kitchener has sustained, all the world over, the ancient valour of the nation, but "peace has her victories no less renowned than war," and little as England has done during the last century compared with what she might have done and ought to have done, it is not too much to say that our progress in true liberty and all beneficent works, in growth of knowledge and at the same time in the extension and stability of the Empire seems more like an Arabian tale than veritable history. And you will find that the greater your knowledge of the century grows, so will the wonder grow also.

How far literature has shared the general advancement it is difficult to say. Civilisation, although a splendid boon, is not without its drawbacks. It is just possible so far as its highest interests are concerned for a nation like an individual to be too well off. In proportion as national progress is confined to the acquisition of wealth, it will be unfavourable to imagina-. tive literature save that which caters to the amusement of the hour. What is great in words is inspired by great deeds, and it may be doubted whether the social com- forts so largely distributed in our day are of such service to the poet as the plain living which Wordsworth associated with high thinking. The love of money is not only the root of all spiritual evil, but it dwarfs the intellect, and when it infects literature renders it, as is perhaps too much the case nowadays, a mere matter of merchandise. Even the student is in danger of regarding that knowledge as of primary importance which is of immediate service instead of loving it disinterestedly and for its own sake. That is the love that yields a lasting reward, and glad shall I be if in any measure I may be able to inspire you with it.

The exquisite poet from whose sonnet upon Chapman's Homer I have taken the title for these Talks, alluded to the poets alone when singing of "The Realm of Gold" in which he had travelled with them; but I think we may make the Realm wider still, and include in it the imaginative prose writers who stand on the border land of poetry, and have enriched the world with beautiful thoughts or created undying characters in fiction. Moreover, the study of the authors who delight and teach by the aid of imagination will lead indirectly to other sources of knowledge supplied by the historian and the biographer. Shakespeare's historical dramas and Scott's historical romances, for example, will lead you, as I have already suggested, to gain further knowledge of the periods described, from the pages of the historian, and after you have reaped delight from Shakespeare and Scott you must be strangely lacking in curiosity if you do not want to learn all that can be known of the men to whom you owe such pleasure.

In order to gain the love of literature, without which books are comparatively worthless, poetry claims our first attention, for the poets when they rightly understand their vocation are our wisest teachers, their song appeals to the heart as well as to the intellect, and their words abiding in the memory yield a joy and solace throughout life.

You will perhaps ask me to define poetry, but that is not in my power. Many definitions have been given from the days of the Greek philosophers to our own, but not one of them is, I think, adequate. Perhaps we should gain little benefit if it were. But if we cannot define poetry there is much about the art which it is not difficult to understand. We cannot fail to see that when the poet, to use Milton's phrase, puts on his " singing robes," he is in a state of exalted feeling in which he sees visions, and is impelled to write what he sees in metre. Profound emotion kindles the imagination and the poet's heart, finds no rest until he is able to express what is stirring within him in a beautiful and lasting form. And we see, too, that while there may be abundant verse without poetry, there can be no poetry, although there may be much that is poetical, without verse. The substance needs also the form, and it is a mistake to speak of the most imaginative prose work as if it were a poem.

No doubt, as an able writer has observed, it is a "disastrous misconception which has made poetry a mere synonym for verse literature of any sort," but it is equally a blunder to suppose that poetry in the strict acceptation of the term is possible without metre. Prose, like verse, has its infinite varieties. It can be gorgeously rhetorical, rich to overflowing in vitality and suggestiveness; it can be simple and forcible, travelling along the beaten roads of life with a clear purpose and with unfailing accuracy; it can be strongly emotional, it can be cold and calm, it can send forth trumpet notes nerving the spirit to battle, it can be tenderly pathetic or run riot with humour. The scope of prose is wide indeed, but the highest inspiration is beyond its reach, and there are thoughts to which no prose can give utterance. This inspiration, these thoughts, find voice in song alone, and if you attempt to translate them into prose their beauty and meaning evaporate. The difference between verse and prose is not one of degree but of kind, and I question whether any one who has been dazzled by the splendour of some enchanting song or subdued by its loveliness can believe that the peculiar influence of which he is conscious could have been produced by prose. Among these so-called prose-poets Thomas De Quincey occupies a prominent place. He thought himself, I believe, and some of his admirers agree in thinking, that the keenest and rarest forms of human feeling may be so expressed in prose as to rival the verse of the lyric poet.

Here is a happy illustration of De Quincey's prose phantasy.   It has an originality and beauty of its own, but is to my thinking as far removed from poetry as the eloquent rhetoric of Burke or the glowing fancy of Jeremy Taylor.

Sweet funeral bells from some incalculable distance, wailing over the dead that die before the dawn, awakened me as I slept in a boat moored to some familiar shore.   The morning twilight even then was breaking; and by the dusky revelations which it spread, I saw a girl adorned with a garland of white roses about her head for some great festival, running along the solitary strand in extremity of haste.   Her running was the running of panic; and often she looked back as to some dreadful enemy in the rear. But when I leaped ashore, and followed on her steps to warn her of a peril in front, alas! from me she fled as from another peril, and vainly I shouted to her of quicksands that lay ahead. Faster and faster she ran ; round a promontory of rocks she wheeled out of sight ; in an instant I also wheeled round it, but only to see the treacherous sands gathering above her head. Already her person was buried ; only the fair young head and the diadem of white roses around it were still visible to the pitying heavens ; and last of all was visible one white marble arm. I saw by the early twilight this fair young head as it was sinking down to darkness— saw this marble arm as it rose above her head and her treacherous grave, tossing, faltering, rising, clutching, as at some false, deceiving hand stretched out from the clouds—saw this marble arm uttering her dying hope, and then uttering her dying despair. The head, the diadem, the arm—these all had sunk ; at last over these also the cruel quicksand had closed ; and no memorial of the fair young girl remained on earth, except my own solitary tears, and the funeral bells from the desert seas, that rising again more softly, sang a requiem over the grave of the buried child and over her blighted dawn. I sat and wept in secret the tears that men have ever given to the memory of those that died before the dawn, and by the treachery of earth, our mother. But suddenly the tears and funeral bells were hushed by a shout as of many nations, and by a roar as from some great king's artillery, advancing rapidly along the valleys and heard afar by echoes from the mountains. " Hush ! " I said, as I bent my ear earthwards to listen ; — " hush ! — this either is the very anarchy of strife or else "—and then I listened more profoundly, and whispered as I raised my head — " or else, oh heavens ! it is *victory* that is final, victory that swallows up all strife."

While impressing on you as I am anxious to do the distinction that must ever exist between verse and prose, I must also ask you to distinguish imaginative prose from the meretricious composition known commonly as "poetical prose." That is generally poor stuff in relation to thought, and invariably false in taste. I think it may be described as due to a superfluous and exuberant use of adjectives, and to a verbosity that runs riot without the help of common sense. There is nothing that bores a reader more than fine talk, and the spinners of flowery prose indulge in it to excess. It is a sickly kind of production born of feebleness (if you wish to see it at its best (or worst) read a book once very popular, *Hervey's Meditations among the Tombs*), and it is totally distinct from the exuberance due to the wealth of fancy that distinguishes great writers like Taylor, Sir Thomas Browne, and Mr. Ruskin, who walk upon the borderland of poetry without trespassing upon it. Taylor's impetuous sweep of imagery, Browne's passionate eloquence, and Ruskin's imperial command of language are no more signs of shallowness than the breeze-ruffled waves of the sea, which conceal ˉ the tranquil depth beneath.

I should like to guard against another misconception into which a youthful reader is likely to fall. English literature has now become a part of scholastic education, and English poets are studied with the minute attention to grammar and syntax which was at one time given only to the classics of Greece and Rome. With this object a play of Shakespeare's is criticised, not for its fine qualities as poetry, but for its verbal peculiarities ; and the perfect music of Milton's *Comus* is dissected in order to discover the poet's idioms and grammatical inflections. To this course of

study no objection can be made, but it
may be easily abused, and will be if the
student imagines that while enlarging his
knowledge of English he is also studying
poetry. That study must be pursued from
the standing-point of literature, not of
grammar ; and it is only through what I
may call literary apprehension that a poet's
work can be understood. If Dryasdust
asks you what poetry proves, you cannot
answer him ; but if once your mind opens
to the inspiration of a tragedy like *King
Lear*, an elegy like *Lycidas*, or to such odes
as that of Keats, *To a Nightingale*, or of
Wordsworth, *On Intimations of Immortality*, you will feel that the imaginative
truth of poetry is as real as a formula of
algebra.

Now let me suppose that you have read
little of the poetry of your country beyond
the pieces published in selections and
perhaps learnt at school, which for that
reason you may hate as Lord Byron hated
Horace. With the chief landmarks of
our poetical history you may be slightly
acquainted, knowing a little about Chaucer
although you have not read his *Canterbury
Tales*, knowing somewhat by report or by
extracts of the luxuriant beauty of Spenser's

Faerie Queene ; knowing how Shakespeare stands among his illustrious contemporaries as Saul stood among the children of Israel, " higher than any of the people "; and how Milton, "the mighty-mouthed inventor of harmonies," fallen upon evil days, nourished his great soul in solitude and blindness.

Darkness before and danger's voice behind.

Then if you have read any history of the Restoration period, Dryden's name will not be unfamiliar, and you will know how this robust writer and consummate master of English, to use his own expressive words, " made prostitute and profligate the Muse."

Probably, too, in your school studies you will have read at least somewhat that has been written about the poets of the last century, and especially of Pope, that exquisite wit and masterly artificer in verse, and of Thomson, whose poetical life was derived from " Nature, the vicar of the Almighty Lord." Then, if your interest has been excited in the subject—and I have been all along taking this interest for granted—you will have heard of the great poetical revolution effected at the beginning of the present century, of which poets like Blake and

c

Burns and Cowper were forerunners in the last. With Coleridge, the most subtly musical of poets, with Wordsworth, the most spiritually suggestive, and with Scott, whose verse, when in his highest mood, is like the tramp of soldiers marching to victory, arose a new era in which, had you lived in it, the poetical figure of Byron would have seemed to you as, to all youthful readers of that time, by far the most prominent, while those of Shelley and Keats, who for intrinsic merit now rank with the peers of song, might have been comparatively disregarded. Then you can recall, perhaps, if you are put through an examination, the names of a score of smaller poets—some of them, like Campbell, Moore, and Rogers, at one time in the highest degree popular—whose fame has now greatly faded.

And bridging over several years in your retrospect, you are, it may be hoped, on familiar ground when calling to mind the finely modulated strains of the latest and the best beloved of deceased Laureates. And yet it is possible, for youthful enthusiasm is not discriminative, and the poetry of the day suits the day, that you are better acquainted with the last idle singer of an

idle lay than with the noblest productions
of a Browning or a Tennyson.

There are, no doubt, exceptions, but I
suppose that, as a rule, the young readers
likely to follow me in these Talks will say
that I have credited them with fully as
much knowledge of English poetry as in
reality they possess.

And now I may be asked, what is the
wisest course a reader should adopt, whose
heart and ear have felt the power of song,
but who is conscious that this love of his,
sincere though it be, is but vague and pur-
poseless, since it is not based upon knowledge? This inquiry I shall endeavour to
answer, premising that the student who
makes it will have already taken a prelimi-
nary step in his journey through this realm,
and will have learned that poetry is not
a mere pastime for leisure hours, but the
highest of intellectual pursuits. And it
is more than this, for it touches a man's
nature at all points. Let me quote what
the greatest of modern poets has to say
upon this subject.

"To be incapable," Wordsworth writes,
"of a feeling of poetry in my sense of the
word, is to be without love of human nature
and reverence for God." And this agrees

with the high estimate of his art formed by Milton, who says that the poet's abilities are the inspired gift of God and are of power (for I must put in a few words what with splendid eloquence he writes at large) " to imbreed in a great people the seeds of virtue and religion." If this be true, the study of the great poets will assuredly bring with it abundant compensation, and although as you grow familiar with them you are not likely to say with Goldsmith that poetry is the source of all your bliss—and this is not to be desired—I believe you will find that it has added a new and lasting joy to life.

SECOND TALK

How shall this study of poetry be begun, and made not a study only but a delight? Unless you can gain pleasure from the pursuit, I know full well that all I may say upon the subject will be thrown away ; some labour you must give, since nothing worth having in this world is to be gained without it, but the compensations are ample, and my endeavour in these Talks will be to show you how beautiful the road is along which we are travelling together, and to give you as few rules as are compatible with progress.

Our poetical literature may be said to have begun with Chaucer, who was born in 1340 and died in 1400, and has in him the glory of youth with all its enjoyment of life and some of its defects. You know the exhilaration of a sunny spring morning when the birds are singing and the fields and hedge-rows bright with flowers. This delightful open-air freshness pervades the verse of Chaucer. He is a master of pathos and of humour, though his humour unfortunately is often very coarse, and he is a master, too, in the delineation of character. Dryden called him "a perpetual fountain of good sense." A man of learning and of excursive reading, he loved books well, and knew how to use without stealing the wealth gleaned from Italy and France. But dearly though he loved books, there were times when he loved nature more, and with a child-like delight would throw them aside to listen to the lark's song or to pluck a daisy from the meadow. He tells us how he gives to books "feyth and ful credence," and how nothing can draw him from them except when in the month of May he sees the flowers and hears the song of the birds, and then with the most charming simplicity he adds :—

> Now have I thanne such a condicioun,
> That of allë the flourës in the mede,
> Thanne love I most thise floures white and rede,
> Suche as men callen daysyes in our toune.
> To hem have I so grete affeccioun
> As I seyde erst, whanne comen is the May,
> That in my bed ther daweth [1] me no day,
> That I nam uppe and walkyng in the mede,
> To seen this floure ayein the sonnë sprede,

[1] Dawneth.

Whan it uprysith erly by the morwe;
That blisful sighte softneth al my sorwe.

In another passage in the same poem, " The Legende of Goode Women," Chaucer once more sings the praise of the flower so dear also to the two greatest of his successors in our century, Wordsworth and Tennyson. He laments that neither in rhyme nor prose can he praise the daisy aright, and tells how with "glad devocioun" he arose before daybreak on the first morn of May to see the flowers unclose :—

And doune on knes anon-ryght I me sette,
And as I koude, this fresshe flour I grette,
Knelyng alwey, til it unclosëd was,
Upon the smalë, softë, swotë gras.

Chaucer knew what the tragedy of life meant, but he generally preferred walking on the sunny side of the road and enjoying heartily all that life has to offer. For more than one reason, but chiefly because I do not want to daunt you with the difficulty of Chaucer's language, although it is but a slight one, I would advise you to leave him alone until a later period. Suppose, then, we pass from the fourteenth century to the sixteenth, and enter the noble realm ruled by Spenser and by Shakespeare.

Before reading the choicest poetry that belongs to this fertile period some acquaintance with the literary history of the age will be of service. You want guidance, for the ways are intricate, and without the use of direction-posts time will be wasted. Gain then at the outset such prominent facts and dates as will show you the relation in which the Elizabethan poets stand to one another, remembering that if a poet is for all time he is also the most faithful representative of his age. There are many text-books that will suffice for the purpose. Mr. Stopford Brooke's primer of literature may help to start you on the road, or you can refer to Mr. Saintsbury's *History of Elizabethan Literature*, a book to be read carefully later on. Of greater help to you perhaps than either will be found the first volume of Mr. Ward's delightful work, *The English Poets. Selections, with Critical Introductions*. Open that volume, and turn to what the late Dean of St. Paul's writes about Spenser, and then read his monograph of this enchanting poet in the series of *English Men of Letters*. Meanwhile take up the *Faerie Queene*, for how can you begin your studies better than by reading " the first great ideal poem that England produced and the source of all our modern poetry " ?

It is written in a stanza called Spenserian, for it is the poet's invention, and shows what a delicate ear for harmony he possessed. Read two or three cantos aloud, so that you may get into the swing of the verse, and do not distract your attention by referring to notes or glossary. What you need at first is to catch the spirit of the poet and the music of his rhythm. Do not be daunted by the extraordinary length of the poem, since the connection of the books is sufficiently slight to allow of their being read separately. If you do not read beyond the first book, which is perhaps the finest, never mind, but I hope you may be impelled onwards, for this " sage and serious poet," as Milton called him, has alluring ways, as many a poet and poetry-lover has discovered. Spenser, " the poet's poet," has proved the guide and joy of nearly all his great successors, and of some true singers who cannot be accounted great.

Cowley, who was born ten years after Milton, writes :

I believe I can tell the particular little chance that filled my head first with such chimes of verse as have never since left ringing there. For I remember when I began to read, and to take some pleasure in it, there was wont to lie in my mother's parlour (I know not by what accident, for she herself never in her life read any book but of devotion), but there was wont to lie Spenser's works. This I happened to fall upon and was infinitely delighted with the stories of the knights, and giants, and monsters, and brave houses which I found everywhere there (though my understanding had little to do with all this), and by degrees with the tinkling of the rhyme and dance of the numbers, so that I think I had read him all over before I was twelve years old, and was thus made a poet.

Dryden, too, calls Spenser "inimitable." He was the delight of Southey and of Scott; and Keats, as Cowden Clarke says, ramped through the scenes of the romance "like a young horse turned into a spring meadow." Nearly all the poets indeed who have sung since Spenser's day tell the same story, and although we, who are not poets, cannot share their fulness of delight, yet in one degree we may find an exquisite and lasting pleasure in the perusal of the *Faerie Queene*. Its wealth of fancy and of imagination is unbounded.

There is sweetness and light in Spenser, and the most prominent characteristic of his verse is beauty. But just as a passing cloud adds charm to a landscape steeped in sunshine, and the shadows of evening are welcome after the unclouded beauty of a summer day, so does the coarse imagery sometimes used by Spenser serve as a foil to the general sweetness of his verse. He lived in a robust age, and is essentially a manly poet. He is not afraid of using plain words which are not always agreeable to read. But the aim throughout his great allegory is the exaltation of virtue and of all things which are lovely and of good report, and this is why he won the praise of Milton for his seriousness, and why John Wesley recommended the *Faerie Queene* to his divinity students. The poem is most discursive, and if you read it in the first instance for the allegory you may be perplexed and irritated. Leave the allegory alone, then, and read the poem for the enchanting music of its verse, for its noble imagination and boundless fancy. Dean Church says, and his judicious criticism always deserves attention :—

At first acquaintance the *Faerie Queene* to many of us has been disappointing. It has

seemed not only antique but artificial. It has
seemed fantastic. It has seemed, we cannot
help avowing, tiresome. It is not till the early
appearances have worn off and we have learned
to make many allowances and to surrender ourselves to the feelings and the standard by which
it claims to affect and govern us, that we really
find under what noble guidance we are proceed-
ing, and what subtle and varied spells are ever
around us.

Now, I think, these sensible words show
that Dean Church must have read the poem
for the first time in mature life and writes
of the effect it exercised at that period. A
young reader, on the contrary, yields to
the spell at once and will not discover in
the poem anything artificial or fantastic.
There is no period of life when those who
have once known and loved Spenser will
turn from him with indifference; but youth
is the season of leisure, and Spenser, even
more than most great poets, demands a dis-
engaged mind open to receive the wealth
which he is able to pour into it. Live then
for a time in his world and its beauty will
gradually open before you. The force of
a great waterfall is at once evident to ear
and eye, but the strength of a mighty river

flowing tranquilly between its banks is not obvious at a glance.

In its brilliant pictures of knights, and fair ladies, and giants, and magicians, the poet's world is unlike our own ; in another sense it is not unreal or remote, for like Spenser's knights we, too, have our battles to fight and our victories to gain at the cost of tears and blood. Spenser, with all his command of imagery, sweetness of rhythm, and joyous out-of-door freshness, is the most serious of poets, and his divine poem, despite some passages, to quote Dean Church's words, of "almost riotous luxuriance," is also a weighty sermon. "No man," it has been justly said, "can read the *Faerie Queene* and be anything but the better for it." You cannot estimate a house from one brick, or a great poem from a few stanzas ; but listen to a short passage which, if it be insufficient to justify the praise of Shelley—and no poet had a finer ear for music—that Spenser's measure is "inexpressibly beautiful," will show you what that measure is. Here is the description of Phædria of the Idle Lake, a pleasure-loving and pleasure-alluring lady who, when Cymochles comes to the water-side, is seen sitting in a "little Gondelay" :—

And therein sate a Lady fresh and fair,
Making sweet solace to herselfe alone :
Sometimes she sang as lowd as larke in ayre,
Sometimes she laught, as merry as Pope Joan ;
Yet was there not with her else any one,
That to her might move cause of merriment :
Matter of merth enough, though there were none,
She could devise ; and thousand waies invent
To feed her foolish humour and vaine jolliment.

Cymochles calls to her to ferry him
across the lake, and the "merry mariner"
turning her boat to the shore admitted him.

Eftsoones her shallow ship away did slide,
More swift than swallow sheres the liquid skye,
Withouten oare or pilot it to guide,
Or winged canvas with the wind to fly :
Only she turned a pin, and by and by
It cut away upon the yielding wave,
Ne cared she her course for to apply ;
For it was taught the way which she would have,
And both from rocks and flats itselfe could wisely save.

Instead of carrying the knight across as
he had desired, she bewitched him with
merry tales and fantastic wit and took him
to her island home.

It was a chosen plot of fertile land,
Emongst wide waves set, like a little nest,
As if it had by Nature's cunning hand
Bene choycely picked out from all the rest,
And laid forth for ensample of the best :

No daintie flowre or herbe that growes on ground,
No arborett with painted blossomes drest
And smelling sweete, but there it might be fownd
To bud out faire and throw her sweete smels all around.

No tree whose braunches did not bravely spring;
No braunch whereon a fine bird did not sitt;
No bird but did her shrill notes sweetely sing;
No song but did containe a lovely ditt.
Trees, braunches, birds, and songs, were framed fitt
For to allure fraile mind to careless ease:
Carelesse the man soone woxe, and his weake witt
Was overcome of thing that did him please;
So pleased did his wrathful purpose faire appease.

With the familiar art of a temptress who turns the bounties of nature to evil uses, Phædria, the Lady of the Idle Lake, incites Cymochles to idleness and pleasure by pointing to the flowers of the field.

Behold, O man! that toilsome paines doest take,
The flowrs, the fields, and all that pleasaunt growes,
How they themselves doe thine ensample make,
Whiles nothing envious nature them forth throwes
Out of her fruitfull lap; how no man knowes,
They spring, they bud, they blossome fresh and faire,
And decke the world with their rich pompous showes;
Yet no man for them taketh paines or care,
Yet no man to them can his carefull paines compare.

The lilly, Lady of the flowring field,
The flower-deluce, her lovely Paramoure,
Bid thee to them thy fruitlesse labors yield,

And soone leave off this toylsome weary stoure :
Loe, loe ! how brave she decks her bounteous boure,
With silkin curtens and gold coverletts,
Therein to shroud her sumptuous Belamoure ;
Yet nether spinnes nor cards, ne cares nor fretts,
But to her mother Nature all her cares she letts.

Why then doest thou, O man ! that of them all
Art Lord, and eke of nature Soveraine
Wilfully make thyselfe a wretched thrall,
And waste thy joyous howres in needelesse paine,
Seeking for daunger and adventures vaine ?
What bootes it al to have, and nothing use ?
Who shall him rew that swimming in the maine
Will die for thrist, and water doth refuse ?
Refuse such fruitlesse toile, and present pleasures chuse.

Spenser, whose faculty of song seems to have been exhaustless, wrote many lovely poems in addition to the *Faerie Queene*, and to him we owe an epithalamic or nuptial song, which is one of the most exquisite outbursts of lyrical genius in the language.

One lovely passage from a lyric that is all loveliness will show you the poet's rhythm in this song. The bride comes into church with trembling steps and humble reverence :—

Behold, whiles she before the altar stands,
Hearing the holy priest that to her speakes,
And blesseth her with his two happy hands,
How the red roses flush up in her cheekes,

And the pure snow with goodly vermill stayne
Like crimsin dyde in grayne :
That even th' Angels, which continually
About the sacred Altare doe remaine,
Forget their service and about her fly,
Ofte peeping in her face, that seems more fayre,
The more they on it stare.
But her sad eyes, still fastened on the ground,
Are governed with goodly modesty,
That suffers not one looke to glaunce awry,
Which may let in a little thought unsownd.
Why blush ye, love, to give to me your hand,
The pledge of all our band !
Sing, ye sweet Angels, Alleluya sing,
That all the woods may answere, and your eccho ring.

Let Spenser but once bewitch you with his verse, and nevermore will you escape from the spell. Not every man, not even every poet—for Landor says Spenser sent him to bed—does this great poet manage to capture. The present age is an impatient one, and some readers will not care to enter a realm so spacious—the *Faerie Queene* alone contains about 35,000 lines — but those who have travelled over this poet's land will find few, if any, of its scenes that do not yield permanent delight. As these are Talks, I may refer to my own experience and recall the days of youth when, with the *Faerie Queene* as my sole companion,

I wandered into the Surrey woods, and throughout one happy leisure day after another read the poem aloud, with no listeners save the birds. Mine was a pocket-edition in six ugly little volumes, but very dear they were to me; and though I have bought more than one fine copy of this great poet since, I almost think I like best the old, coarsely-printed volumes that remind me of my youth and of golden joys. The poem, as I have before observed, is an allegory, which, as Dean Church says, "bodies forth the trials which beset the life of man in all conditions and at all times." Do not be afraid of reading it on that account. The meaning that lies beneath the surface may interest you later on; at first you will do well not to trouble about it. Read this most ravishing of all poetical romances simply for its poetry, and if its music does not enter into the heart, there will be some reason to fear that very much I may have to say to you about the poets will be listened to as a foreign and but half-familiar tongue.

"The general end of all the book," says its author, "is to fashion a gentleman or noble person in virtuous and gentle discipline, which for that I conceived should be

most plausible and pleasing being coloured
with an historical fiction, I chose the history
of King Arthur."

The final portion of the *Faerie Queene*
was published in 1596, and it is interesting
to remember that forty-two years later, when
Milton was nine-and-twenty, he thought of
taking up the Arthurian legend as the
subject for an epic poem ; a theme so nobly
treated by one of the worthiest of Spenser's
successors, a poet very dear to all Englishmen—Alfred Tennyson.

Spenser was the friend of Sir Walter
Raleigh, to whom he dedicates one of
his poems, and also of Sir Philip Sidney,
whose brief life, like that of the longer
and far sadder life of Raleigh, lives
in English history. When Sidney died,
England felt that she had lost her ideal
knight, the most perfect soldier and gentleman of the Court of Queen Elizabeth.
More than 200 elegies or orations were
written or uttered in his honour, one of
which was from the pen of Spenser, "and
it was accounted sin," says a biographer,
"for any gentleman of quality for many
months after to appear at Court or city in
a light or gaudy apparel." Sir Philip's
early passion for "Stella"—Lady Penelope

Devereux—had been marred by the poor girl's enforced marriage to Lord Rich, a man of bad character; but Sidney did not cease on that account to make love to her in poetry, after the fashion of the age. His verse, like his prose romance *Arcadia*, is full of conceits, but it has also much beauty of a high order, many dainty turns of expression, many sweetly harmonious lines. Whether the lady in her maiden state returned Sidney's love we do not know, and there is no reason to believe that she did so when enduring the neglect of her unkind husband. Truth to the facts of biography is not the mark of love poetry in Elizabeth's age, nor indeed in any other, and you might as well look for it in the labyrinthine pages of Sidney's *Arcadia* as in his sonnets. Some of these sonnets are very beautiful. Spenser, Sidney, and Shakespeare are the first three poets of note in the line of our sonnet writers, and in this subtle art I think that Sidney surpasses Spenser. The sonnet is a noble form of poetry, but its rhythmical complexity and its condensation are not fitted to please readers who are making their earliest travel in the Realms of Gold. At the same time it is well you should know that nearly all our most famous poets have added a fresh laurel wreath to their crown by this form of verse, and it is well to mark as we pass along, some features of the country, which when you grow older may excite greater interest.

Of all our poets Shakespeare is not only the greatest but by far the best known, since his dramas are acted as well as read. Like Nature herself, the riches of Shakespeare seem inexhaustible. You know probably that his age was as much that of the drama as ours is of the novel, and that he stands surrounded by a crowd of brother dramatists, some of whom were greatly gifted poets. It was an age of song too, and in all our literature there is not to be found more lyrical beauty than in the Elizabethan and Jacobean periods. In this exquisite art Shakespeare is also supreme, and it is this fulness of power in the two highest regions of poetry that excites the wonder of the student. And there is a third characteristic in which Shakespeare stands far above his fellows. The dramatists of the time are as remarkable for grossness as for poetic vigour, and often, like their successors of the Restoration period, may be said to hold a brief for vice. Shakespeare can be coarse, sometimes offensively so, but he never sneers at what is sacred, never treats virtue with contempt, or writes as if there were no distinction between right and wrong. His atmosphere is one in which healthy people can breathe. Let me advise you to gain at least a familiar knowledge of a few of this supreme poet's masterpieces—of *Hamlet*, *Macbeth*, *Lear*, and *Romeo and Juliet* in tragedy; of *Twelfth Night*, *Merchant of Venice*, and *As You Like It* in comedy; of the *Midsummer Night's Dream* and *The Tempest* in that marvellous region of Shakespeare's art, which seems to belong to neither; and of *Henry V.*, *Julius Cæsar*, and *Richard III*. in the historical drama. And when these dramas have become a portion of your poetical heritage you will still find more worlds to explore which this myriad-minded man has created. In addition to the creative power of the imagination, of music, and of fancy, gifts peculiarly poetical, you will find that his pages teem with wise sayings, expressed in so happy a form that what he says in this way has become part of our colloquial language. We are apt indeed to think Shakespeare and to speak Shakespeare, so that with the single exception of the Authorised Version of the Scriptures there is no English book that has contributed so greatly to the common speech of Englishmen. Some of the noblest thoughts in Shakespeare come from woman's lips—the noblest and the sweetest. No poet has recognised as he has done all that is best and truest and most divine in the character of womán or maiden, wife and mother. Shakespeare is a dramatist, and therefore does but slightly reveal his own personality, but his love of country is more clearly expressed than by any English poets, save Wordsworth, Tennyson, and Scott.

> This England never did, nor never shall
> Lie at the proud foot of a conqueror,

and

> Nought shall make us rue
> If England to itself do rest but true,

express a spirit which, in spite of political divisions and some internal discord, has knit the country into one body whenever the fear of invasion has called forth its strength. In the drama which contains the noble couplet

> All places that the eye of heaven visits
> Are to a wise man ports and happy havens!

you will find also the immortal lines, which, like Scott's

Breathes there the man with soul so dead,

cannot be read without the glow of patriotism :—

This royal throne of kings, this sceptred isle,
This earth of majesty, this seat of Mars,
This other Eden, demi-paradise ;
This fortress built by Nature for herself
Against infection and the hand of war ;
This happy breed of men, this little world,
This precious stone set in the silver sea,
Which serves it in the office of a wall,
Or as a moat defensive to a house,
Against the envy of less happier lands ;
This blessed spot, this earth, this realm, this England,
        .   .   .   .   .   .
This land of such dear souls, this dear, dear land,
Dear for her reputation through the world.

The student of any art will always do well to build up his knowledge by studying its greatest masters.   Yet I would not confine your attention to the most illustrious of the Elizabethans, a term which for convenience sake may extend to Milton.   What variety and force there is in Michael Drayton, to whom we owe our most beautiful love sonnet and finest battle-song! what poetic wisdom and mastery of style in Samuel Daniel, the "well-languaged Daniel"! what brightness, although often dimmed by grossness, in the sparkling songs of Herrick! what rare lyrics in *The Forest and Underwoods* of Ben Jonson! what tenderness of feeling and buoyancy of spirit in the smoothly-flowing verse of George Wither! Here is indeed ample delight provided for all who know how to enjoy it, but it will be a delight not wholly unalloyed.

Such poets as Ben Jonson and Robert Herrick must be praised with large reservations. Some of Jonson's lyrics are of choice beauty, having in them the freshness of spring and the perfume and warmth of summer, while others are ignoble in thought and often faulty in expression. If you read Herrick in the selection made by Mr. Palgrave you will find little that is not pure gold, but this old poet's worth and worthlessness are pretty equally divided in the works which when an old man, and a clergyman also, he did not scruple to publish. As a rural poet he is delightful, as a singer of love lyrics he sometimes almost reaches the highest level, but as a writer of epigrams

The Realms of Gold

Herrick, like his friend Ben Jonson, often sinks to the lowest. There are few things worse of the kind or more contemptible in our literature. George Wither, on the contrary, wrote nothing to be ashamed of from a moral point of view, but he wrote a good deal that is amazingly feeble; and if you walk with him in the Realms of Gold, as you may do pleasantly for a brief stroll, his Muse, should you follow her much longer, would quickly carry you into the dullest region of prose. The tiny volume that contains Wither's "Fair Virtue" and the "Shepherds' Hunting" will show you that Wither, whose fault is that of too great a fluency, has the poet's gift; and how dearly he loved his Art is seen in the following lines written when he was in prison:—

Poesy, thou sweetest content
That e'er Heaven to mortals lent:
Though they as a trifle leave thee,
Whose dull thoughts cannot conceive thee,
Though thou be to them a scorn,
That to nought but earth are born,
Let my life no longer be
Than I am in love with thee,
Though our wise ones call thee madness,
Let me never taste of gladness,
If I love not thy maddest fits
Above all their greatest wits.

And though some, too seeming holy,
Do account thy raptures folly,
Thou dost teach me to contemn
What makes knaves and fools of them.

It would be an interesting amusement by the way, and something more than an amusement, to collect all the beautiful things in verse or prose which our English poets have said about the Art they love. To do so might need some labour from students whose knowledge of our poetical literature is limited, but it would prove, I think, a toil closely linked to delight. Shakespeare, the greatest of dramatists, writes admirably on this as on most subjects, but the poet who has written the most nobly about it in prose is Milton, whose majestic language when he touches on this theme is worthy of the author of *Paradise Lost*. And the place where this exaltation of the poet's art is to be found makes it the more significant. Milton was a strong and indeed a scurrilous controversialist in an age of controversy. Too often in place of argument, like an angry child, he calls names, but even in his fighting mood and amidst the din of polemical warfare he will suddenly lay aside his weapons and, sitting down in green pastures and by peaceful waters, will talk with his readers of his high hopes as a poet and of how, to use an old-fashioned phrase, he had dedicated his life to the service of the Muses. The finest and fullest of these passages is to be found in Book II. of *The Reason of Church Government urged against Prelacy;* but there is another and highly character-istic passage in the pamphlet entitled *An Apology for Smectymnuus*, in which, while vindicating his personal character, he relates that he had even from youth upwards loved those poets best who displayed "sublime and pure thoughts without transgression," and had become confirmed in the opinion "that he who would not be frustrate of his hope to write well hereafter in laudable things ought himself to be a true poem; that is, a composition and pattern of the best and honourablest things, not presuming to sing high praises of heroic men or famous cities unless he have in himself the experi-ence and the practice of all that which is praiseworthy."

Drayton's *Polyolbion,* a long poem in which he makes a poetical journey through England, interesting though it be, is not a poem even for youthful leisure; and his *Barons' Wars*, in spite of Ben Jonson's praise and of its merits, may be passed by without loss. History in verse, unless it be treated as Shakespeare treats it by the help of the drama, is profitable to neither poet nor reader. Drayton, strange to say, was alive to his friend Daniel's weak point, saying that he was "too much historian in verse," and appears to have been unaware of a similar defect in his own *Barons' Wars*. But both Daniel and Drayton are true poets, as you will some day find when you read Daniel's noble poem in defence of learning,[1] and his *Epistle to the Countess of Cumberland*, "composed," says Wordsworth, "in a strain of meditative morality more dignified and affecting than anything of the kind I ever read," and Drayton's charming *Nymphidia* and also his Agincourt ballad. Stay, why should you not listen to that spirit-stirring ballad now? You cannot but like it, and I think remember it too, so full of fire are its manly stanzas.

Fair stood the wind for France
When we our sails advance,
Nor now to prove our chance
Longer will tarry,

[1] Samuel Daniel had a keen sense of the glory of poetry by which men "live two lives where others live but one," and exclaims :

What good is like to this
To do worthy the writing, and to write
Worthy the reading and the world's delight?

But putting to the main,
At Kaux, the mouth of Seine,
With all his martial train,
    Landed King Harry.

And taking many a fort,
Furnish'd in warlike sort,
Marcheth towards Agincourt
    In happy hour,
Skirmishing day by day
With those that stopp'd his way,
Where the French gen'ral lay
    With all his power.

Which in his height of pride,
King Henry to deride,
His ransom to provide
    To the king sending.
Which he neglects the while
As from a nation vile,
Yet with an angry smile
    Their fall portending.

And turning to his men,
Quoth our brave Henry then:
"Though they to one be ten
    Be not amazed.
Yet have we well begun,
Battles so bravely won
Have ever to the sun
    By fame been raised.

"And for myself (quoth he)
This my full rest shall be,
England ne'er mourn for me;
    Nor more esteem me:

Victor I will remain,
Or on this earth lie slain,
Never shall She sustain
    Loss to redeem me.

" Poitiers and Cressy tell
When most their pride did swell,
Under our swords they fell:
    No less our skill is
Than when our grandsire great,
Claiming the regal seat,
By many a warlike feat
    Lopped the French lilies."

The Duke of York so dread,
The eager vaward led;
With the main Henry sped
    Amongst his henchmen.
Excester had the rear,
A braver man not there,
O Lord, how hot they were
    On the false Frenchmen !

They now to fight are gone,
Armour on armour shone,
Drum now to drum did groan,
    To hear was wonder;
That with the cries they make
The very earth did shake,
Trumpet to trumpet spake
    Thunder to thunder.

Well it thine age became,
O noble Erpingham,
Which didst the signal aim
    To our hid forces;

64 The Realms of Gold

When from a meadow by,
Like a storm suddenly,
The English archery
  Stuck the French horses,

With Spanish yew so strong,
Arrows a cloth-yard long,
That like to serpents stung
  Piercing the weather;
None from his fellow starts,
But playing manly parts,
And like true English hearts,
  Stuck close together.

When down their bows they threw,
And forth their bilbows drew,
And on the French they flew,
  Not one was tardy;
Arms were from shoulders sent,
Scalps to the teeth were rent,
Down the French peasants went,
  Our men were hardy!

This while our noble king,
His broad sword brandishing,
Down the French host did ding
  As to o'erwhelm it.
And many a deep wound lent,
His arms with blood besprent,
And many a cruel dent,
  Bruisèd his helmet.

Gloster, that duke so good,
Next of the royal blood,
For famous England stood
  With his brave brother.

Clarence, in steel so bright,
Though but a maiden knight,
Yet in that furious fight
  Scarce such another

Warwick in blood did wade,
Oxford the foe invade,
And cruel slaughter made,
  Still as they ran up.
Suffolk his axe did ply,
Beaumont and Willoughby,
Bare them right doughtily,
  Ferrers and Fanhope

Upon Saint Crispin's day
Fought with this noble fray,
Which fame did not delay
  To England to carry.
Oh, when shall Englishmen
With such acts fill a pen,
Or England breed again
  Such a King Harry?

When Shakespeare died, John Milton, his greatest successor in our English Realm of Gold, was a child of eight. As he grew to manhood he devoted himself to poetry as the noblest of vocations, trusting, to quote his own words, "that what the greatest and choicest wits of Athens, Rome, or modern Italy, and those Hebrews of old did for their country, I, in my proportion, with this over and above, of being a

E

Christian, may do for mine." How nobly he fulfilled the purpose of his early manhood his great epics testify. Truly does Wordsworth say that his soul "was like a star and dwelt apart." In the most dissolute age of our history, in poverty and solitude, Milton breathed the air of heaven, and was permitted to see and tell

> Of things invisible to mortal sight.

We are most of us afraid of enthusiasm in these days, but it is difficult to avoid giving expression to it while listening to the "organ-voice of England." It has been well said that the knowledge a man brings home after foreign travel depends in large degree on the supply he carried out. The same remark holds good, I think, with regard to such poems as *Paradise Lost* and *Paradise Regained.* The more a reader knows of the art, and of the chief poets of antiquity, the more will he appreciate the consummate skill with which Milton has used his learning, drawing gold from all sources, and yet so transmuting the precious metal that it becomes his own. Before studying these masterpieces, written in old age and blindness, it is well to learn what a perfect voice of song Milton possessed in his youth when he wrote *Comus*, *Lycidas*, *L'Allegro*, *Il Penseroso*, and that great Hymn on the Nativity which has in it lines unsurpassed in force and imagery even by Milton himself. Ben Jonson wrote some admirable masques, but the only verse of the kind that has taken an enduring place in literature is *Comus*, a poem which may well be called divine, not only because it reaches the highest water-mark of poetry, but for its lofty and Christ-like purity. "That virtue," writes Mr. Masson, "will always in the long run beat vice even in this world, unless the whole frame of things is rottenness, God a delusion, and the world not worth living in or dying in, or thinking about—ransack all Milton's writings from the very earliest and this will be found, in one form or another, the idea ever deepest with him and most frequently recurring." This is true of *Comus*, but how much more might be said in praise of a poem that would suffice of itself to give Milton a proud rank among his country's poets. Then there is *Lycidas*, which, in spite of much lovely verse of the same character written in later times, still stands, I think, at the head of our elegiac poetry. Add to these the two descriptive poems, as perfect of their kind, and we have a small volume of poetry unsurpassed in the rareness of its quality by any youthful poet. Here, indeed, are "infinite riches in a little room," and free to all who value beauty and truth.

It has been said that *Paradise Lost* and *Paradise Regained* are more talked about than read. It may be so, but I am sure that no reader who has once felt the inspiration of Milton's genius can ever neglect them. Henceforth they become a portion of his intellectual life. No poet has used the English language with the sustained harmony of Milton. Sublimity of imagination and an exquisite ear for rhythm are this poet's chief characteristics, and in these great qualities he has never been surpassed. The advice I gave with regard to Spenser may be followed also with Milton. Read him at first as Dr. Johnson advised people to read Shakespeare, with a disregard of the commentators. There may be much that you will not understand, but there will be very much to enjoy. A further study of the poems, which abound with the literary knowledge of which the poet was master, can be left to a second perusal.

Paradise Lost was published in 1667, and in 1678, four years after Milton's death, a volume appeared with which it is probable you are more familiar. We talk, and rightly, of a poet's inspiration, but if ever book was inspired it is John Bunyan's prose allegory, *The Pilgrim's Progress.* That is a narrative which concerns every one, and its imaginative beauty can be felt by all of us. It was written with the fervour of a man who had seen the things that are unseen, both in the depths and in the heights, had fought with spiritual foes, had now lived in "Doubting Castle," and now walked in green pastures, had groped his fearful way through the dark valley, and had stood on the Delectable Mountains companied by ministering spirits who "walk the earth unseen both when we sleep and when we wake."

I suppose that next to the Bible there has been no book more read than this marvellous allegory, and the fine Saxon diction in which it is written makes it as welcome to the homeliest reader as to the man of high culture.[1] It is a volume for all seasons and for all periods of life, but it has a special charm for those who come to its pages with

---

[1] A foolish attempt has been lately made to translate *The Pilgrim's Progress* into modern English, and it is almost needless to say that much of its charm is lost in the process.

fresh and unsophisticated minds. *The Pilgrim's Progress* is, as Lord Macaulay justly says, "the only work of its kind which possesses a strong human interest. Other allegories only amuse the fancy. The allegory of Bunyan has been read by many thousands with tears." John Bunyan, who was originally a tinker, became a very popular minister among the Baptists. He suffered imprisonment for his faith under the sway of the careless, pleasure-loving, and most contemptible of all our monarchs, Charles II. Jeremy Taylor, who was Bunyan's senior by fifteen years, and had been chaplain to Charles I., also learned what it was to be persecuted for conscience sake when the Puritans were in the ascendant. At the Restoration he was made a Bishop, but it was in his retirement and poverty in Wales that he wrote the great works that have made him immortal. Of these the choicest and the dearest is his *Rules of Holy Living and Dying*, a book which has been truly called a divine pastoral. Its sweet persuasiveness, its tender winning appeals, its gentle wisdom, and the glowing richness of its style, give Jeremy Taylor's *Rules* a place in our heart and on our shelves very near to that occupied by the *Pilgrim*. Both indeed are household volumes bound together by the golden cord of love and noble seriousness. Otherwise no works could be more unlike. Taylor's exuberant fancy, his vast knowledge, and his illustrations borrowed from all sources, form a striking contrast to the simple eloquence and robust diction of Bunyan. But both men with the same purpose in view have written books that can be taken up again and again with pleasure and from which the best kind of wisdom is to be gained. Much of the delight to be received from the *Pilgrim* and the *Holy Living* is due to the vivifying force of the imagination,—to that lifting power that teaches, while it inspires, and this is why I ask you to receive them as companions and friends.

If I read to you a passage or two from these great writers it will make a break in our "Talk" that may be pleasant to all of us. Here is a protest against vain fear from one of Taylor's sermons :—

I have often seen young and unskilful persons sitting in a little boat, when every little wave sporting about the sides of the vessel and every motion and dancing of the barge seemed a danger, and made them cling fast upon their fellows, and yet all the while they were as safe as if they sat under a tree while a gentle wind shook the leaves into a refreshment and a cooling shade; and the unskilful inexperienced Christian shrieks out whenever his vessel shakes, thinking it always a danger that the watery pavement is not stable and resident like a rock, and yet all his danger is in himself, none at all from without; for he is indeed moving upon the waters but fastened to a rock; faith is his foundation, and hope is his anchor, and death is his harbour, and Christ is his pilot, and heaven is his country, and all the evils of poverty or affronts of tribunals or evil judges, of fears and sadder apprehensions, are but like a loud wind blowing from the right point; they make a noise and drive faster to the harbour; and if we do not leave the ship and leap into the sea, quit the interests of religion, and run to the securities of the world, cut our cables and dissolve our hopes, grow impatient and hug a wave and die in the embraces, we are as safe at sea, safer in the storm which God sends us than in a calm when we are befriended with the world.

Another characteristic passage was written when the author was living among friends in his pleasant exile :—

I am fallen into the hands of publicans and sequestrators, and they have taken all from me; what now? Let me look about me. They have left me the sun and moon, fire and water, a loving wife and many friends to pity me, and some to relieve me and I can still discourse, and unless I list, they have not taken away my merry countenance and my cheerful spirit and a good conscience; they still have left me the providence of God and all the promises of the Gospel, and my religion and my hopes of heaven and my charity to them too; and still I sleep and digest, I eat and drink, I read and meditate; I can walk in my neighbours' pleasant fields and see the variety of natural beauties and delight in all that in which God delights—that is, in virtue and wisdom, in the whole creation and in God Himself. And he that has so many causes of joy and so great is very much in love with sorrow and peevishness, who loses all these pleasures and chooses to sit down upon his little handful of thorns. Such a person is fit to bear Nero company in his funereal sorrow for the loss of one of Poppea's hairs or help to mourn for Lesbia's sparrow.

Taylor's fancy is often so rampant that he indulges in grotesque allusions like that which I have just quoted. Writing in *Holy*

Living of the good that is to be gained out of evil he says :—

When the north wind blows hard and it rains sadly, none but fools sit down in it and cry; wise people defend themselves against it with a warm garment or a good fire and a dry roof. When a storm of a sad mischance beats upon our spirits . . . it will turn into something that is good if we list to make it so.   He that threw a stone at a dog and hit his cruel stepmother said that although he intended it otherwise yet the stone was not quite lost ; and if we fail in the first design, if we bring it home to another equally to content us, or more to profit us, we have put our conditions past the power of chance.

Some grave readers may blame such quaint sayings as trivial, but in Taylor they are not out of harmony with the deepest seriousness of thought.   " The most poetical of divines," as I have said elsewhere, "is also one of the weightiest.   If he rambles to pluck flowers by the way, he has always the cunning art of extracting from them medicine and fragrance." [1]

" Love," he writes, " is the greatest thing that God can give us, for Himself is love, and it is the greatest thing we can give to

[1] *Jeremy Taylor's Golden Sayings*, edited by J. Dennis.   Innes and Co.

God, for it will also give ourselves, and carry with it all that is ours "; and very beautifully does he illustrate this divine charity by the following story which he found " in the Jews' books " :—

When Abraham sat at his tent door, according to his custom, waiting to entertain strangers, he espied an old man stooping and leaning on his staff weary with age and travel coming towards him, who was a hundred years of age. He received him kindly, washed his feet, provided supper, and caused him to sit down ; but observing that the old man eat and prayed not, nor begged for a blessing on his meat, he asked him why he did not worship the God of heaven. The old man told him that he worshipped fire only and acknowledged no other god ; at which answer Abraham grew so zealously angry that he thrust the old man out of his tent and exposed him to all the evils of the night and an unguarded condition. When the old man was gone, God called to Abraham and asked him where the stranger was. He replied, " I thrust him away because he did not worship Thee." God answered him, " I have suffered him these hundred years although he dishonoured Me, and couldst not thou endure him one night, when he gave thee no trouble ? " Upon this, saith the story, Abraham fetched him back again and gave

him hospitable entertainment and wise instruc-
tion.   Go thou and do likewise, and thy charity
will be rewarded by the God of Abraham.

From Bunyan I select a passage from
the First Part of *The Pilgrim's Progress,*
when Christian's journey is over and he is
approaching the home that he has so long
desired.   The whole story of his passage
through the river with his friend Hopeful
is written with what might be called consummate art, were it not that in Bunyan's
case it was the expression in unpremeditated
and inspired words of the writer's innermost
belief :—

Now while they were thus drawing towards
the Gate, behold a company of the Heavenly
Host came out to meet them : to whom it was
said, by the other two shining Ones, These are the
men that have loved our Lord, when they were
in the World ; and that have left all for his Holy
Name, and he hath sent us to fetch them, and
we have brought them thus far on their desired
Journey ; that they may go in and look their
Redeemer in the face with joy.   Then the
Heavenly Host gave a great shout, saying,
*Blessed are they that are called to the Marriage
supper of the Lamb.*   There came out also at

this time to meet them several of the King's Trumpeters, cloathed in white and shining Raiment, who with melodious noises and loud made even the Heavens to echo with their sound. These Trumpeters saluted Christian and his Fellow with ten thousand welcomes from the world; And this they did with shouting and sound of trumpet.

This done, they compassed them round on every side; some went before, some behind, and some on the right hand, some on the left, (as 'twere to guard them through the upper regions,) continually sounding as they went, with melodious noise, in notes on high; so that the very sight was to them that could behold it as if Heaven itself was come down to meet them. Thus therefore they walked on together; and, as they walked, ever and anon these Trumpeters, even with joyful sound, would, by mixing their Musick with looks and gestures, still signify to Christian and his Brother how welcome they were into their company, and with what gladness they came to meet them. And now were these two men, as 'twere, in Heaven, before they came at it, being swallowed up with the sight of Angels, and with hearing of their melodious notes. Here also they had the City itself in view; and they thought they heard all the bells therein to ring, to welcome them thereto. . . . Oh! by what tongue or pen can their glorious joy be expressed : Thus they came up to the Gate.

Now when they were come up to the Gate, there was written over it, in Letters of Gold, *Blessed are they that do his commandments, that they may have right to the Tree of life ; and may enter in through the Gates into the City.*

Then I saw in my dream, that the shining men bid them call at the Gate, the which when they did, some from above looked over the Gate ; to wit, Enoch, Moses, and Elijah, &c., to whom it was said, These Pilgrims are come from the city of Destruction, for the love that they bear to the King of this place : and then the Pilgrims gave in unto them each man his Certificate, which they had received in the beginning ; those therefore were carried in to the King, who when he had read them, said, Where are the men ?   To whom it was answered, They are standing without the Gate.   The King then commanded to open the Gate ; *That the righteous Nation*, said he, *that keepeth Truth may enter in.*

Now I saw in my Dream, that these two men went in at the Gate ; and lo, as they entered, they were transfigured, and they had raiment put on that shone like Gold.   There was also that met them with Harps and Crowns, and gave them to them ; the Harps to praise withal, and the Crowns in token of honour; Then I heard in my Dream that all the bells in the City rang again for joy: and that it was said unto them, *Enter ye into the joy of your Lord.* I also heard the men themselves, that they sang with a loud voice, saying, *Blessing, Honour, Glory and Power, be to him that sitteth upon the Throne, and to the Lamb for ever and ever.*

Now just as the Gates were opened to let in the men, I looked in after them; and behold, the City shone like the Sun, the Streets also were paved with Gold, and in them walked many men, with Crowns on their heads, Palms in their hands, and golden Harps to sing praises withal.

There were also of them that had wings, and they answered one another without intermission, saying, *Holy, Holy, Holy, is the Lord.* And after that, they shut up the Gates: which when I had seen, I wished myself among them.

Two sacred poets much and deservedly loved belong to this period, I mean George Herbert and Henry Vaughan, the latter being nearly thirty years Herbert's junior, and the more imaginative of the two. I will not say much about them, for their quaintness may repel young readers, but both are born poets, and both will some day, I hope, win your love, for they well deserve it. You might, however, with advantage and pleasure too, read the beautiful life of Herbert as recorded by Izaak Walton, a name dear to all anglers, and I will add to all good men ; and if you do not care as yet to read Herbert's *Temple*, the pithy verses which introduce it may arrest your attention. And there is a sonnet of Herbert's upon Sin which I shall like to quote, for it contains in fourteen lines one of the weightiest of sermons :—

Lord, with what care hast Thou begirt us round !
Parents first season us ; then schoolmasters
Deliver us to laws ; they send us, bound
To rules of reason, holy messengers,
Pulpits and Sundays, sorrow dogging sin,
Afflictions sorted, anguish of all sizes
Fine nets and stratagems to catch us in,
Bibles laid open, millions of surprises ;
Blessings beforehand, ties of gratefulness,
The sound of glory ringing in our ears,
Without, our shame ; within, our consciences ;
Angels and grace, eternal hopes and fears.
Yet all these fences and their whole array
One cunning bosom-sin blows quite away.

Milton is the supreme poet of the seventeenth century, but there was more than one poet in his day who enjoyed a greater popularity. John Dryden, who wrote of *Paradise Lost* as " undoubtedly one of the greatest, most noble and sublime poems which either this age or nation has produced "—he should have said any age or nation—was, so the story runs, styled by Milton "a rhymer but no poet." If Milton said it he might be excused, since none of the great satires upon which the fame of Dryden chiefly rests appeared before Milton's death.   As a rhetorical and didactic poet he holds a high place in literature, but he has written none of the essentially imaginative poetry which attracts and ought to attract the young.

Some day you will probably read his *Absalom and Achitophel*, his *Hind and Panther*, and *The Fables.   Alexander's Feast*, a great lyrical effort, may be known to you already, since it is to be found in most selections.   There is, however, only one point in relation to Dryden to which I shall ask your attention now.   As a prose writer he may be called the father of modern English.   Dryden was Milton's junior by twenty-three years.   Both were splendid masters of prose.   Milton is sublime and strong, with a force that sweeps everything before it ; he writes with an elevation and fervour which is with difficulty restricted by the rules of grammar and syntax; his words have frequently the grandeur of prophetic utterances and also the obscurity; he wields the language as he pleases; his resources seem to be exhaustless, and he uses them like a giant. There is no blank verse in the language that can be compared with Milton's for harmony; there is perhaps no prose that can compare with his for force. But Milton's involved sentences and gorgeous diction are not fitted for daily service, and Dryden, in his Prefaces and Essays, has shown us how to write what may be called the prose of common life.

 No matter upon what subject the poet writes, there is everywhere the same manly simplicity and purity of idiom, and it is not too much to say that every distinguished writer of good English since Dryden's day has learnt some lessons in his school. He was Pope's master in verse, and I think he was Swift's master in prose. If he was not the first author of the seventeenth century who wrote in a plain style, he was the first, unless an exception is made in favour of Cowley, to use that style with beauty and precision.

Abraham Cowley, as I have said already,

was Milton's contemporary, and the popular
taste of the age preferred him as a poet.
His verse, though often that of a true
poet, swarms with conceits which caught
the fancy of the time, but the little volume
of his Essays shows that in prose he knew
what simplicity was, though in verse he
wandered far astray. He died seven years
before the death of Milton and was buried
in Westminster Abbey, an honour, I need
scarcely tell you, of which the far greater
author of *Paradise Lost* was not accounted
worthy. It will, perhaps, amuse you to
hear that Waller, another popular poet
of the age, spoke of Milton's great epic
as being remarkable for nothing but its
extreme length, a criticism which may
suggest to you, if you do not know it
already, that critics are not infallible.
Another striking illustration of this fact is
the judgment of Edmund Waller's contemporaries, that he was one of the greatest,
if not the greatest, of English poets. " He
first made writing easily an art," Dryden
said, and the chief merit that distinguishes
his verse is the ease with which it flows.
Waller is well-nigh forgotten now save for
one or two lyrics, but the following lovely
lines, composed when the poet was over

eighty and on his death-bed, deserve to be
remembered :—

> The seas are quiet when the winds give o'er !
> So calm are we, when passions are no more !
> For then we know how vain it was to boast
> Of fleeting things, so certain to be lost.
> The soul's dark cottage, batter'd and decay'd,
> Lets in new light through chinks that time has made ;
> Stronger by weakness, wiser men become,
> As they draw near to their eternal home ;
> Leaving the old, both worlds at once they view
> That stand upon the threshold of the new.

THIRD TALK

JOHN DRYDEN died in 1700, William Cowper died in 1800. The century was one of great literary activity, but it failed until its closing years to produce a highly imaginative poet. The voice of song was comparatively silent, and Pope, who for a long period reigned without a rival, could not sing at all. It has been called, not inaptly, the "Age of Prose," and whatever poetical energy it possessed was carefully restrained by the curb of common sense. You will find much to interest you, however, in several of the eighteenth-century authors, although the literary tone of the age is more remarkable for wit than for imaginative art.

Some of the sweetest fancies were struck out by the essayists, who introduced a new form of literature, and a form that made itself welcome to all readers. "The Town,"

however, as London was then called, formed
the whole world to authors, and they scarcely
seemed to know anything even of the rural
beauty lying within a few miles of Charing
Cross.   Defoe, the earliest English novelist,
had travelled over the country, and in his
prosaic fashion describes very vividly what
he saw, but his descriptions display small
perception of natural beauty, and the finest
mountain scenery was to him "barbarous
and frightful."   His novels, with perhaps
the sole exception of *Robinson Crusoe*, are
remarkable for qualities that are the reverse
of poetical.   He was full of invention, but
destitute of romance; you scarcely know
how to believe that you are reading fiction,
since Defoe is careful to impress upon
you that he is the humble chronicler of
familiar facts.   His first object is to deceive
his readers, and in this cunning art he is
without a rival.   So apparently trustworthy
is his *History of the Plague*, "written by
a citizen who continued all the while in
London," and "lived without Aldgate Church
and Whitechapel Bars on the left hand or
north side of the street," that a well-known
physician of that age quoted the book as an
authority.   *Robinson Crusoe* stands alone
among Defoe's novels.   It is a matchless

book of its kind, and one which cannot fail to delight every boy-reader ; but I cannot agree with the opinion of an accomplished critic, that it is "one of the most beautiful of the world's romances." Many fine qualities it has, but I do not think that "beauty" is a striking characteristic of *Robinson Crusoe*. If it were, the book would not cease to charm when the days of youth are over.

Defoe's own life was one of the strangest versatility. He could write on almost any subject and he could represent almost any character. He was at one time a tradesman, at another the busiest and least scrupulous of party journalists ; he was one day the most pious of moralists and outspoken of reformers, and anon is discovered acting the shameless part of a government spy. He suffered in the pillory for defending religious liberty, and spoke out boldly against the evils of the age, yet he lied with energy all his life long, and exerted every kind of ingenuity to escape from his creditors. He could make sacrifice for principle, and he could act as if he had lost the sense of right. Like his own Crusoe, Defoe lived a solitary life, and was disregarded or disliked by the men of letters who ruled the town in the days of "good Queen Anne" and of George I.

Addison and Steele, whose names must be always linked together, were two of the most prominent.   They are the first English essayists who found material for their humour in the foibles and fashions of the age, and to them, though in a lesser degree than to Defoe, we are indebted for originating the novel of common life as distinguished from the heroic and interminable romances of earlier times.   Their essays, which are to be found chiefly in the *Tatler* and *Spectator*, may appear tame to readers accustomed to browse on sensational fiction; but you, I hope, wish to understand the difference between books that live for the hour and books that have in them an enduring charm, and therefore I recommend you to read the choicest papers of these brother essayists, and to discover if you can the secret of their once amazing popularity. This was partly due to the fact that they were, as Dr. Johnson quaintly says, "among the first books by which both sexes were initiated in the elegancies of knowledge." Addison's humour is exquisite, and his style, in its gentle attractiveness, is perfect ; Steele is often careless, but he is sprightly and pathetic, and the story of his life and love-making, I may say in passing, explains the merits and the defects of his literary work. Happy was the man who wrote fairly good poetry or prose in the days of Queen Anne! Addison on the wings of verse that would not be envied by a third-rate poetaster in our day rose to be Secretary of State. No doubt he deserved his honours, for he was a fine scholar, a man of great ability and of the highest integrity, but even Addison's enemies—and virtuous though he was he had some, Pope being the most prominent and dangerous—do not seem to have suspected that he was not a poet, for in those days small poetical mercies were gratefully accepted. He is, however, a delightful humorist, and if you do not already know his *Sir Roger de Coverley*, I advise you to make the acquaintance of that worthy knight and of his friends without delay.

Lord Macaulay wrote an admirable essay on Addison, in which, by the way, he is very unjust to Steele, and in that essay he recommends certain papers in the *Spectator* as illustrative of Addison's genius :—

It is dangerous to select (he writes) where

there is so much that deserves the highest praise. We will venture, however, to say that any person who wishes to form a just notion of the extent and variety of Addison's powers will do well to read at one sitting the following papers :—" The Two Visits to the Abbey," " The Visit to the Exchange," " The Journal of the Retired Citizen," " The Vision of Mirza," " The Transmigrations of Pug the Monkey," and " The Death of Sir Roger de Coverley."[1]

Readers, and especially young readers, find it of service to be guided, and I am sure you cannot spend the time more pleasantly than in following the course prescribed by Macaulay. At the same time, do not wholly neglect Steele. He is a far less faultless writer, but he is so human, so lively, so full of sympathy that, for my part, there are times when Addison's perfect workmanship has less of charm than the glowing feeling and natural eloquence of Sir Richard. He was full of faults, but I will show you by one brief anecdote how much he was beloved. In 1713 Steele took his seat in Parliament as M.P. for Stockbridge, and had no sooner taken his seat

---

[1] The *Spectator*, Nos. 26, 329, 69, 317, 159, 343, 517.

than he was accused of sedition as the author of a political pamphlet which the Tories considered an inflammatory libel. He was called upon for his defence and spoke for three hours. When he left the House several members defended Steele, and among them was Lord Finch, whose sister had been attacked in a Tory paper for " Knotting in St. James's Chapel during divine service in the immediate presence both of God and Her Majesty who were affronted together." Steele had replied with some sharpness in his paper, *The Guardian*, and defended the lady from calumny.

Like Steele, Lord Finch was a new member; and when Steele was assailed for party purposes, the young nobleman sprang to his legs for the first time in defence of the man who had done his sister a kindness. His generous impulse seemed for the moment more generous than wise. The speaker hesitated, was overcome by timidity, and sat down exclaiming, " It is strange I cannot speak for this man, though I could readily fight for him." A cheer filled the House at these loyal words, and Lord Finch, with his courage revived, rose a second time, and is said to have made a capital speech. It was a gallant but vain effort, for Steele lost his seat by a large majority.[1]

Steele, who died in 1729, had a thousand weaknesses and a thousand charms besides. An impulsive, open-hearted Irishman, he reminds us of another Irishman, far more famous and still dearer, who was born in Dublin one year before Sir Richard's death. You will guess I mean Oliver Goldsmith, who, though not one of the greatest, is one of the best beloved of English poets. The story of his strange adventurous life has been admirably told by more than one biographer. It reads like a romance and ends, as so many poet's lives have ended, in a tragedy. The strange and, it is to be feared, true stories told about him are innumerable. How he proposed to seek his fortune in America and spent all his money before reaching the ship; how a good uncle endowed him with fifty pounds, that he might study law in England, and how he lost it all for the second time before leaving Dublin; how, having rejected one profession, he proposed to study another,

---

[1] I quote from an essay on Steele which appeared several years ago in the *Cornhill* and was afterwards reprinted in my *Studies of English Literature*.

and was sent by way of a third experi-
ment to Edinburgh as a medical student;
how from thence the future poet went to
Leyden, which he quitted "with only one
clean shirt and no money in his pocket."
How then, like his own George Primrose
in *The Vicar of Wakefield*, he is supposed to
have wandered about Europe earning food
and a night's lodging by playing on a flute;
and how, after a year of wandering, he
landed at Dover with only a few pence in
his pockets. Whether he played his way
to London we are not told. In that great
city, and "without," as he says, "friends,
recommendations, money, or impudence,"
he was sore bestead. For a while he
assisted an apothecary, and afterwards, by
the help of an old college friend, started on
his own account in a humble way. It
would seem that few patients entrusted
their lives to Goldsmith, and ere long he
became usher in a school. Teaching, however, proved as impossible a profession as
medicine. After more than one more effort
and disappointment, he found his vocation
as a bookseller's hack and commenced his
labours in a garret. "He was a plant that
flowered late," said Dr. Johnson, who had
fought his own way to fame through the

deepest poverty and distress before he paid his first visit to Goldsmith in 1761. How one would like to have been present at that memorable supper when Johnson, to the surprise of a companion, adorned himself in a new wig and a new suit of clothes. " I hear," he said, "that Goldsmith, who is a very great sloven, justifies his disregard of cleanliness and decency by quoting my practice, and I am desirous this night to show him a better example." Goldsmith may have been slovenly, but at the same time he cherished a secret passion for showy garments, as the bills of his friendly tailor Filby still exist to testify. I must not detain you with this lovable man and delightful writer, who, as Dr. Johnson says on the monument raised to his memory in Westminster Abbey, "touched nothing that he did not adorn." What I want you to do is to read the poet's biography and his sweet and graceful verse. For charm and for an exquisite art that reads as if it were artless, I know nothing better than *The Traveller* and *The Deserted Village*, and as to *The Vicar of Wakefield*, its witchery as an imaginative prose idyl has now for more than a century taken captive innumerable readers. The poet Goethe said that the book came to him at a critical moment in his mental development and proved his best education. This, if you are familiar with the tale, may excite your wonder, but a poet receives what he gives, and might well gain more from the homely wisdom and sweet charity of the romance than they are likely to yield us.

In *The Citizen of the World*, a volume published when Goldsmith was thirty-four, a Chinese philosopher relates his adventures to friends in the Far East. The book has many passages that foretell the humour which afterwards blossomed more freely in the narrative of Dr. Primrose. In *The Deserted Village* there is, as you doubtless know, an exquisite portrait of a country parson. Here is another in prose :—

Poor as he was, he had his flatterers still poorer than himself; for every dinner he gave them they returned an equivalent in praise, and this was all he wanted. The same ambition that actuates a monarch at the head of an army influenced my father at the head of his table. He told the story of the ivy tree, and that was laughed at; he repeated the jest of the two scholars and one pair of breeches, and the company laughed at that; but the story of Taffy in the sedan chair was sure to set the table in a roar. Thus his pleasure increased in proportion to the pleasure he gave; he loved all the world, and he fancied all the world loved him.   As his fortune was but small, he lived up to the very extent of it; he had no intentions of leaving his children money, for that was dross; he was resolved they should have learning, for learning, he used to observe, was better than silver or gold.   For this purpose he undertook to instruct us himself, and took as much pains to form our morals as to improve our understanding.   We were taught to consider all the wants of mankind our own . . . in a word, we were perfectly instructed in the art of giving away thousands before we were taught the more necessary qualifications of getting a farthing.

I have often wished that the poet Gray, who died three years before Goldsmith, had recorded his opinion of the Vicar, and that Goldsmith, who had reviewed Gray's *Odes*, had told us what he thought of his *Elegy*, which is declared to be, and yet who is qualified to say, the most popular poem in the language.   There are some eccentric critics and poetical compilers nowadays who esteem it of small worth, but it lives in the heart and memory of every true lover of poetry.

Gray had the odd fancy that his *Elegy* owed its great popularity to the subject, and would have been liked as well had it been written in prose. We may be sure that, however artfully the work had been done, it would have been forgotten long ago. It is the verse that preserves the thought to us and keeps it as fresh as on the day it was first written.

Try, for instance, to put the fifth and sixth stanzas into prose, and you will soon discover the folly of such an effort. Nay, if you placed them in the hands of a great master of English, he would tell you that the task was too hard for him.

> The breezy call of incense-breathing morn,
>   The swallow twitt'ring from the straw-built shed,
> The cock's shrill clarion, or the echoing horn,
>   No more shall rouse them from their lowly bed.

> For them no more the blazing hearth shall burn,
>   Or busy housewife ply her evening care ;
> No children run to lisp their sire's return,
>   Or climb his knees the envied kiss to share.

There is much about Gray that attracts us. Like Pope, the lonely Cambridge student was devoted to his mother, and had, one may guess, deeper feelings than he cared often to express. He was a very

learned man, and possessed, what learning
does not give, the art of writing charming
letters. Then he discovered and drank
in with delight the witchery of mountain
scenery, and was indeed one of the earliest
writers of his century who showed the love
of natural beauty which we all feel in the
present day, or are supposed to feel. It
was Gray who first described the beauty
of the Lake country, now for ever to be
associated with the names of Wordsworth,
Southey, and Coleridge, and with other
names second indeed to theirs, but far
from insignificant in the annals of literature.
Our earlier travellers felt no admiration
for a region that was to them "savage wild."
Thomas Fuller, a quaintly, witty author,
whose acquaintance you will make some
day, said there was cold comfort from Nature
in Westmoreland; Defoe calls it the most
frightful and barbarous country of any which
he had seen; and Gilpin, another eighteenth-
century traveller, describes one of the fairest
valleys in Cumberland as "replete with
hideous grandeur." Gray, on the other hand,
not only writes with rapture of our English lakes, but, after returning from a visit
to Scotland, says : "I am charmed with my
expedition; it is of the Highlands I speak;

the Lowlands are worth seeing once, but the mountains are ecstatic and ought to be visited in pilgrimage once a year." To Gray, a shy and sensitive man, Nature seems to have been dearer than society. Mountains, lakes, and rivers opened his heart and gave life to his pen. Like Gilbert White of Selborne, he was familiar with the habits of birds and flowers, and there was no object too small to enlist his sympathy. To the grander features of this wonderful world he was, as I have said, equally susceptible. The secret charms of Nature are revealed to early risers, and here is the description of a sight that enchanted Gray very early on an autumnal morning as he stood by the seaside :—

I saw the clouds and dark vapours open gradually to right and left, rolling over one another in great smoky wreaths, and the tide as it flowed gently in upon the sands, first whitening, then slightly tinged with gold and blue ; and all at once a little line of insufferable brightness that (before I can write these few words) was grown to half an orb, and now to a whole one, too glorious to be distinctly seen. It is very odd it makes no figure on paper ; yet I shall remember it as long as the sun, or at least as long as I endure. I wonder whether anybody ever saw it before! I hardly believe it.

"The pomp and prodigality of heaven," to use Gray's noble words, although not in his sense, were ever a joy and delight to him; and one day, after wandering by Derwentwater, he wrote :—

In the evening walked alone down to the Lake by the side of Crow Park after sunset, and saw the solemn colouring of light draw on, the last gleam of sunshine fading away on the hilltops, the deep serene of the waters, and the long shadows of the mountains thrown across them, till they nearly touched the hithermost shore. At distance heard the murmur of many waterfalls not audible in the daytime. Wished for the moon, but she was *dark to me and silent*, *hid in her vacant interlunar cave.*

I read this passage to you, because it anticipates the feeling that inspired Wordsworth, and in his measure Coleridge, thirty years later. If you were to look through the five volumes of Pope's *Correspondence* you would not find an intimation from him or from any of his distinguished friends that the solemn charm of Nature in her lonely paths had been felt to inspire and subdue. The words of Gray would have been incomprehensible to Swift or Gay, to Bolingbroke or Arbuthnot, and neither Cowper, who was daunted by " the tremendous height of the Sussex hills," nor perhaps even Gray would have fully understood Coleridge's passion when he wrote :—

I never find myself alone within the embracement of rocks and hills . . . but my spirit careers, drives, and eddies like a leaf in autumn ; a wild activity of thoughts, imaginations, feelings, and impulses of motion rises up within me. . . . The further I ascend from animated nature, the greater in me becomes the intensity of the feeling of life.

The passion for mountain-climbing is a growth of our century, partly, no doubt, because facilities of travel make mountains more accessible ; and partly from the stimulus excited by poets like Byron and Wordsworth. Byron made them the burden of much of his verse in *Manfred* and *Childe Harold*, and sometimes dilates on this favourite theme with great exaggeration ; as, for example, when he asks whether he should not contemn all objects if compared with the mountains, waves, and skies :—

Are not the mountains, waves, and skies, a part
Of me and of my soul, as I of them ?
Is not the love of these deep in my heart
With a pure passion ? should I not contemn
All objects, if compared with these, and stem
A tide of suffering rather than forego
Such feelings for the hard and worldly phlegm
Of those whose eyes are only turn'd below,
Gazing upon the ground, with thoughts which dare
　　not glow ?

Wordsworth loved Nature more deeply, and assuredly more wisely since, profoundly as he felt the influence of the scenery amidst which he lived, he cared more for humanity than for the loveliest of inanimate objects. Nature, apart from human life, may gladden a poet's eye but does not fully satisfy his heart.　And it is worth noting, by the way, how the poets and prose writers alike never show for long the enthusiasm aroused by natural objects without giving to those objects a meaning and a sympathy which belong not to them but to ourselves.　Mr. Ruskin calls this the " Pathetic Fallacy," and illustrates his meaning by a quotation from Kingsley :—

They rowed her in across the rolling foam—
The cruel, crawling foam.

" The foam," he says, " is not cruel, neither does it crawl," and he observes that the falseness in our impressions of external things is produced by "violent," and, I suppose, therefore ill-regulated feelings. I cannot think this judgment a correct one. The feelings of the poet or of the poetically imaginative writer may be strong without being violent, and when he is thus moved, it seems inevitable that the Nature with which these feelings are associated should be represented as sharing in them. Coleridge asserts this when he says :—

> We receive but what we give,
> And in our life alone does Nature live ;
> Ours is her wedding garment, ours her shroud !

It may seem presumptuous to say that Nature lives only in our life, when we remember that "millions of spiritual creatures walk the earth unseen" for whom Nature has no shroud ; but so long as we bear the burden of humanity Nature must bear it also, and whatever we say of her in our higher moods is said for the most part in the language which we apply to ourselves. This is a necessity from which Mr. Ruskin himself cannot escape. Thus, for instance, writing about trees he says :—

> The resources of trees are not developed until they have difficulty to contend with ; neither

their tenderness of brotherly love and harmony, till they are forced to choose their ways of various life where there is contracted room for them talking to each other with their restrained branches.

And in another place, writing of a pine forest in the Jura, he gives a personal and powerful illustration of the way in which the beauty or the desolation of Nature is dependent on human feeling :—

I came out presently on the edge of the ravine ; the solemn murmur of its waters rose suddenly from beneath, mixed with the singing of the thrushes among the pine boughs ; and on the opposite side of the valley, walled all along as it was by grey cliffs of limestone, there was a hawk sailing slowly off their brow, touching them nearly with his wings, and with the shadows of the pines flickering upon his plumage from above, but with a fall of a hundred fathoms under his breast, and the curling pools of the green river gliding and glittering dizzily beneath him, their foam globes moving with him as he flew. It would be difficult to conceive a scene less dependent upon any other interest than that of its own secluded and serious beauty ; but the writer well remembers the sudden blankness and chill which were cast upon it when he en-

deavoured, in order more strictly to arrive at
the sources of its impressiveness, to imagine it,
for a moment, a scene in some aboriginal forest
of the New Continent.   The flowers in an
instant lost their light, the river its music ; the
hills became oppressively desolate ; a heaviness
in the boughs of the darkened forest showed
how much of their former power had been
dependent upon a life which was not theirs, how
much of the glory of the imperishable, or continually renewed creation, is reflected from things
more precious in their memories than it, in its
renewing.   Those ever springing flowers and
ever flowing streams had been dyed by the deep
colours of human endurance, valour and virtue ;
and the crests of the sable hills that rose against
the evening sky received a deeper worship, because their far shadows fell eastward over the
iron wall of Joux and the four-square keep of
Granson.

And now, after reading this beautiful
passage, I may ask whether it is more of
a pathetic fallacy to write of "cruel foam"
than of the hills becoming in an instant
"oppressively desolate," and of the forest
boughs as overtaken with "heaviness"?
Among recent Englishmen no one has
studied Nature in her different aspects more

lovingly or written of her more beautifully than Ruskin. He is justly dear to the young, for he loves and understands them, and to them in several of his works he has rendered the supreme service of being at once instructive and inspiring. No modern author has better appreciated the superlative force and beauty of our language, or has used it with a fuller sense of responsibility.

The poet Gray's love of Nature has led me naturally enough to leap over more than a century, but it would have been difficult to speak of mountain scenery without thinking of Mr. Ruskin whose imagination has been more kindled by the wonder and glory of these "high places" than that of any other prose writer.

Gray, apart from his *Elegy*, was never a popular poet, but those who knew his art best appreciated him warmly. " I think him," Cowper writes (but he must have forgotten Milton for the moment), "the only poet since Shakespeare entitled to the character of sublime."

It was not until fourteen years after Gray's death that Cowper published *The Task* and became, as Southey says, the most popular poet of his generation. In him we have a poet eminently truthful and direct. He looked straight at Nature, and if his interpretation of what he saw is not profound like that of his great successor Wordsworth, it is always honest. *The Task* appeared in 1785. About half a century earlier James Thomson had published *The Seasons*, a descriptive poem of kindred character, but with some fine features and some striking faults not to be found in Cowper's quieter and more domestic poem. Apart from the *Elegy* and the *Night Thoughts* of Young these poems were the most popular produced in the last century. The fact is remarkable, since both Thomson and Cowper are poets of the country, and all their loveliest passages are transcripts of Nature as seen with a poet's eye. The age, on the contrary, was one in which Nature was slighted for Art, and if we except his knowledge of landscape gardening, Pope, who was the poetical lawgiver of the period, might, so far as Nature is concerned, have lived all his life within four walls.

The Task is, I fear, no longer familiar, yet it is not a poem to be neglected, for Cowper is a true poet, and here we have some of his best work. To him Nature was so dear that the simplest objects please and suffice to yield inspiration. In this he resembles Wordsworth; but apart from their different modes of looking at Nature you will observe one striking difference between them. Cowper, one of the saddest of men, has an abundant sense of humour; Wordsworth, by his own confession, one of the happiest, has none. Many other points of contrast might be mentioned, but this will suffice. Read Southey's Biography of Cowper, a charming book, written in the perfect style of which Southey was a master, and you will see how completely the poet's verse is the outcome of his life. He is the poet of the family, and like Longfellow, is never so happy as when he keeps near the hearth or describes the familiar rural scenery, half-village and half-country, that surrounds the home. The fine gold of poetry is mixed in Cowper's case with a great deal of dross, and owing to his sad mental state, some of his religious views are morbid. In his case much may be left unread; but to appreciate Cowper it would be well to become acquainted with *Charity*, *Conversation*, and *Retirement*, with Books IV., V., and VI. of *The Task*, with the lines *To my Mother's Picture*, and with the verses addressed to Mary Unwin, the dear and faithful companion of his sad life. The tragical pathos of *The Castaway*, the exuberant mirth of *John Gilpin*, and the considerable success Cowper achieved as a translator of Homer show the versatility of this poet's genius. And you will see it still more when you come to read his letters. "I once thought Swift's letters the best that could be written," Cowper said, "but I like Gray's better. His humour, or his wit, or whatever it is to be called, is never ill-natured or offensive; and yet, I think, equally poignant with the Dean's." The last century was famous for its letter writers, but I think Gray would deserve the palm were it not for Cowper, who, in a style quite inimitable and obviously unstudied, writes of himself and of his friends as he would have talked over the table at Olney.

Before passing to the greatest British poet of the century, I must remind you that long ere the arrival of a supreme singer in Burns, several minor but genuine lyric poets had flourished whose voices had charmed his ear. Some of the best of these singers were women. Jean Adams wrote the famous song, "There's nae luck about the house." Isabel Pagan wrote "Ca' the yowes to the knowes,"—"a

beautiful song in the true old Scotch taste,"
is Burns's criticism of it; Jane Elliot and
Mrs. Cockburn both wrote the "Flowers
of the forest," and the reader of the two
versions will probably find it hard to say
which he likes the most. Lady Baillie, too,
wrote "Werena my heart licht I wad dee";
and in Burns's own day Lady Nairne and
Lady Anne Lindsay—witness her incomparable "Auld Robin Gray"—added in no
mean measure to the fame of Scottish song.

In 1786 Burns published the volume of
poems that was destined to secure his fame.
Cowper a year later read the book twice
and pronounced it "a very extraordinary
production." He thought it a pity the
poet did not write "pure English," which
perhaps from Cowper was not so strange a
regret as it seems to readers of Burns in
our day. But he observes, with a true feeling for the Scotch ploughman's genius:
"He is, I believe, the only poet these
kingdoms have produced in the lower rank
of life since Shakespeare (I should rather
say since Prior) who need not be indebted
for any part of his praise to a charitable
consideration of his origin and the dis-
advantages under which he has laboured."
Again Cowper writes that he despairs of

meeting with any Englishman who will take the pains that we have taken to understand him : "His candle is bright, but shut up in a dark lantern."

This was probably an objection the greater number of English readers would have made when the little volume found its way over the Border, but not many perhaps at that early period would have praised the poet so generously. Cowper, however, did not see what every one sees now, that Burns was never thoroughly true to his genius, save when he wrote in his native dialect.

In his purely English poems and in his correspondence he is often highly artificial. Burns stands in the front rank of song writers, never surpassed, and, considering the variety as well as merit of his lyrics, it is not too much to say never equalled. Much indeed he gleaned from his Scottish predecessors, but he changed all he touched with the certainty and supreme power of genius :—

> Through busiest street and loneliest glen
> Are felt the flashes of his pen :
> He rules 'mid winter snows, and when
>   Bees fill their hives :
> Deep in the general heart of men
>   His power survives.

It is interesting to note the sympathy of this robust poet with the smallest of God's creatures—with the mouse that he disturbed with his plough, and with poor Mailie, his "only pet yowe." No poet who had not an almost feminine tenderness for his fellow-mortals in the field could have written poems like these. His pathos, like his humour, is always genuine, and finds a direct road to the heart. To remember how Burns sometimes desecrated his transcendent genius, and while seeing with clearest vision what was right, followed what was wrong, is among the saddest of poetical recollections. Genius is no excuse for vice, and the light that leads astray is not from heaven; but men and women who have no genius are just as liable to fall as Burns, just as guilty if they do fall, and there is not one of us whose consciousness of weakness should not force him to say

> The best of what we do and are,
> Just God, forgive.

Before leaving the eighteenth century behind us, I must talk to you a little about one of the most famous books and men which that century produced.

Samuel Johnson was born in 1709 when Pope was one-and-twenty and when Steele and Addison were writing in the *Tatler;* he died in 1784, two years after Cowper had published his first volume of poems.   His life, therefore, covered a vast period of which he may be accounted the literary dictator. He held a unique position.   There have been far greater critics since Johnson's day, deeper thinkers, men who have taken a more comprehensive view of literature and of life, but there is not one, I do not except even Coleridge or Carlyle, who sits in the chair assigned by his contemporaries to Dr. Johnson.   Indeed, the times are so altered, and the world of letters so expanded, that there is no longer room for an autocrat in the realm of letters.   Nowadays it is not so much Johnson's writings that keep his memory green as his character, and that character, with all its virtues and failings, is presented to us in one of the most delightful books in the language.

The interest of Boswell's *Life of Dr. Johnson* is inexhaustible, and in reading it you will make the acquaintance of most of the famous men and women who lived during the years in which Johnson occupied a first place in the literary society

of London. No man could have held literature in higher honour, and few Englishmen
have done more to make it worthy of
esteem. He thought that a nation derives
its highest reputation from the splendour
and dignity of its authors, and he wrote
in the belief that it lay with him to add
something to that dignity and splendour.
The story of a great and good man con-
fronting difficulties bravely and coming out
of them victorious is always inspiriting, but
this famous *Life* has also for students of
literature an historical value. It is a revela-
tion of Johnson's age from the literary
standpoint and explains, with singular clearness, its weaknesses, its limitations, and its
strength. Dr. Johnson, who wrote poems
himself, and very good they are of their
kind, won high repute in his own day as
a critic of imaginative literature, and his
most famous book, as you are doubtless
aware, is *The Lives of the Poets*. One of
the peculiarities of this significant work is
that more than half of the men honoured
by Johnson's notice were versemen and
not poets. They "rhymed and rattled"
and thought they were producing poetry;
Johnson was aware in most instances that
they were not, but he wrote under order from

the booksellers who knew the men whose works were likely to sell best, for these *Lives* were written to accompany an edition of the *English Poets.* The booksellers' judgment, a sound one no doubt financially, shows therefore to the student what the taste of the age was in matters poetical.

Twenty years ago Mr. Matthew Arnold published a volume containing six of these famous Lives, namely, those of Milton, Dryden, Swift, Addison, Pope, and Gray, and in his preface he explains so admirably the value of such a work, though I cannot agree with the limitation he has set on its worth, that it would be a folly to use any words of my own, so well has he said already what I wish to say.

A student cannot read them (he writes) without gaining from them consciously or unconsciously an insight into the history of English literature and life. He would find great benefit, let me add, from reading in con-nexion with each biography something of the author with whom it deals : the first two books, say, of *Paradise Lost* in connexion with the Life of Milton ; *Absalom and Achitophel,* and *The Dedication of the Æneid* in connexion with the Life of Dryden ; in connexion with Swift's Life, *The Battle of the Books ;* with Addison's,

The Coverley Papers ; with Pope's, *The Imitations of the Satires and Epistles of Horace.* The *Elegy in a Country Churchyard* everybody knows, and will have it present to his mind when he reads the Life of Gray. But of the other works which I have mentioned[1] how little can this be said ; to how many of us are Pope and Addison and Dryden and Swift and even Milton himself mere names about whose date and history and supposed characteristics of style we may have learnt by rote something from a hand-book, but of the real men and of the power of their works we know nothing ! From Johnson's biographies the student will get a sense of what the real men were, and with this sense fresh in his mind he will find the occasion‧propitious for acquiring also, in the way pointed out, a sense of the power of their works.

The Lives of the Poets is, I think, an eminently suggestive book throughout. With many critical errors, it is rich in practical wisdom and leads the reader by pleasant ways along many varied tracks of literature. Johnson was himself ever eager for knowledge, and his *Lives* are not limited to poetical criticism. Even the opposition some

[1] Mr. Arnold is alluding to the *Lives* not included in his selection.

of his statements will excite is not without its value. He generally gives a reason for his literary creed, and the biography of the most insignificant poetaster is illuminated by flashes of the author's genius. Dr. Johnson was one of those burdened men who feel the sorrows of life more keenly than its pleasures. He wrote a poem on the *Vanity of Human Wishes*, and his one prose tale, *Rasselas*, is on the same theme, a story far more remarkable for weighty sayings than for incident. It is very solemn and very sad, but so powerfully written that it rapidly became a popular work and was translated into several languages.

The fund of thinking (Boswell writes) which this work contains, is such that almost every sentence of it may furnish a subject of long meditation. I am not satisfied if a year passes without my having read it through, and at every perusal my admiration of the mind which produced it is so highly raised, that I can scarcely believe that I had the honour of enjoying the intimacy of such a man.

Boswell was a hero-worshipper, and his critical judgment is by no means equal to his craft as a biographer. He was full of follies which excited Johnson's mirth, but

Boswell knew how to make use of his own weaknesses, and by exhibiting them as no sensitive man could have done, he enhances his master's merit. We laugh at him as Johnson laughed and are grateful for the mirth that he affords. Lord Macaulay endeavours to make out that Boswell was a man of the feeblest and meanest intellect; and Macaulay being one of the most popular of writers, many of his readers, and you perhaps may be among the number, have accepted the famous essayist's decision. But Macaulay loved to make a statement effective by exaggeration, and the fact which he admits that Boswell has written the best biography in the language will suffice to prove that, however glaring his faults may have been, it was not because he was "a great fool" that he became "a great writer."

FOURTH TALK

I HAVE now tried to give you, though very imperfectly, a glimpse of our English Realm of Gold from the imperial sway of potentates like Spenser and Shakespeare to the century that closes with the powerful voice of Burns and the gentler influence of Cowper. To know the country well that owns men like these as legitimate sovereigns will need months and even years of delightful travel ; but it is something to know a little how the land lies, and if I have been able to lead you on a few roads, or at least while acting as a sign-post, to point in the right direction, my task will not be a vain one. But I feel that this slight service will be useless, unless I can inspire you with enthusiasm for this noble study which above all others demands feeling as well as knowledge.

The works that are based on the imagination whether in verse or prose, form the high-water mark of literature and show us, if I may apply Milton's words, "The bright countenance of truth in the quiet and still air of delightful studies." There are many readers able in some degree to appreciate the imagination that blossoms in prose who do not in the least understand the still higher claim on their regard that is legitimately made by the poet.

Now, if any one were to ask me, "What is the use of poetry?" I should be inclined to answer, "Of none whatever at present to you, my friend." There must be some force of passion in order to appreciate, however inadequately, a poet's ardour, some glow of imagination in order to yield due reverence to his supreme power, and if ever you are conscious of this passion and of this imaginative fire, you will no longer ask, "What is the use of poetry?"

And yet I will not answer your question quite so abruptly, but will reply to it in the first place by asking another question: What is the use of the beauty that gladdens us in the eyes of women, that enchants us in every aspect of Nature; the exhaustless variety of colour in vegetation, the splendour of sunsets, the "many twinkling smile" of the sea? Why is the ear charmed by the song of birds, by the happy voices of children, by the stream leaping over the rocks, and why does the sight of that stream, those children, and those rocks fill the mind with pleasure? We cannot explain, perhaps, the aversion caused by ugliness, or why beauty holds us captive, but there are few people so uncultured as to have no sense, though it may be but a faint one of the power of loveliness, whether physical or moral. Poetry is the embodiment of this sense of beauty in the most perfect form of words, and is written when the poet is carried above himself. In those supreme moments, rhythm is as necessary to him as colour to the artist and form to the sculptor. In its degree, also, you will find it necessary to the imaginative prose writer who, when inspired by his theme, falls into a balance and harmony eminently grateful to the ear.

One use, then, of poetry is to afford delight. There is another. The noblest wisdom is seen by the light of the imagination and the true poet is the seer. We cannot, neither can he, explain his inspiration, but it is certain that his greatest utterances are not dependent on his will. He cannot sit down and say, "Now I will write poetry"; he cannot command his thoughts, they command him. Moreover, while imaginative art gives us delight and wisdom, it also supplies a soothing power which is of priceless value in the struggle of life. When that admirable man, F. W. Robertson of Brighton, was worn by suffering, and to use his own expressive word, "shattered," he wrote :—

In a literary point of view I find Sir Walter Scott the best restorative of any. There was no morbid spot in that strong, manly heart and nature.

Coleridge said that poetry had ever been to him its own exceeding great reward, and Wordsworth regarded it as the object of his poems "to console the afflicted, to add sunshine to daylight by making the happy happier; to teach the young and the gracious of every age to see, to think and feel, and therefore to become more actively and securely virtuous." And now, I think, I have shown you what the service rendered by poetry is, if we have but heart enough and brain enough to make good use of it.

It may not be evident to every young student of poetry that popularity is no test of merit. Poems of slight value or of none have, for some temporary reason, had a great reputation with uncritical readers, and then, after a few years, have taken their place among the books that nobody reads. In the history of English poetry, you will find several striking illustrations of this truth. I will give one which may serve as a starting-point for what I have to say about the poets and imaginative writers of this century. In 1792 Samuel Rogers published *The Pleasures of Memory*, and in six years that mellifluous but vapid poem had reached ten editions. So highly did Byron think of Rogers's art that he ranked him above Coleridge and Wordsworth. At the present day Rogers, if not quite dead as a poet, is chiefly to be remembered for having preceded the great poets who flourished in the first half of this century, and for having survived them all. On the other hand, during long years Wordsworth was the most unpopular poet in England.

Coleridge, whose name is "second to none of all time for splendour and sweetness of inspiration," was laughed to scorn by the early critics of his verse, and Keats was unsparingly ridiculed in the *Quarterly*. Yet these three poets stand now in the front rank, while some of the poets of that day who, like Moore, made fame and money by their verses, are seldom read.

Another poet of far higher mark than Thomas Moore is, it may be feared, equally neglected, I mean George Crabbe. He belongs to the past century, as well as to the present, for the first poem which gained him a place in literature was published in 1781, one year before Cowper's appearance as a poet, and the *Tales of the Hall* in 1819. In early life he enjoyed the friendship and generous patronage of Burke; in later life he was the friend of Wordsworth and of Scott, and from them, as well as from Southey, and from Lord Byron who called him

Nature's sternest painter and her best,

received no stinted praise. To Sir Walter Scott, Crabbe's poetry was a perpetual delight, and like the famous statesman Charles Fox, he asked that it might be read to him in his dying hours. In recent days two men, wholly unlike in intellect and character — Cardinal Newman and Mr. Swinburne—have expressed the same admiration for this singularly original poet; Lord Tennyson, too, added his voice to this chorus of praise, so that, although

Crabbe is comparatively neglected by the public, you will see that he is not without the " fit audience " which a poet loves best. Now what has he done to make him in the best sense of the word famous ?   On a hasty perusal the reader is likely to be more conscious of his defects than of his merits, for he is frequently perverse, careless, and indeed often conspicuously prosaic. The parody of Crabbe's style in that amusing book, *Rejected Addresses*, is scarcely an exaggeration when the spirit of poetry has forsaken him.   That parody opens with the following lines :—

> John Frederick William Alexander Dwyer
> Was footman to Justinian Stubbs, Esq.,
> But when John Dwyer enlisted in the Blues,
> Emanuel Jennings polished Stubbs's shoes.

Now this sounds a little overstrained even for a parody, but listen to the poet himself, who begins one of his tales with :—

> Grave Jonas Kindred, Sybil Kindred's sire,
> Was six feet high and looked six inches higher.

And another with :—

> Counter and Clubb were men in trade, whose pains
> Credit and prudence brought them constant gains ;
> Partners and punctual every friend agreed
> Counter and Clubb were men who must succeed.

It would be impossible to find anything in verse more abjectly prosaic, and there are many such passages in Crabbe, but he is a true poet notwithstanding, and has, as Lord Tennyson once said, " A world of his own," and an original genius "which entitles the possessor to what we call immortality." No modern poet has seen with clearer eyes the weaknesses of men and the gloomier aspects of Nature, and his severe but one-sided truthfulness in the delineation of character will probably have little charm for you, since, as a wise critic has said, it takes the bloom from life. On the whole, his poetry is not elevating, but there are passages in it not to be surpassed for pathos and for vividness of description. Careless of language, he is fertile of ideas, and the solid virtues of his poetry will show you how boundless are the realms of verse, when in our English territory a poet like Crabbe belongs to the royal blood as surely as Milton or as Keats. Shakespeare writes of a homely country life as one of sweet content ; the lyric poets of the seventeenth century delight in praising pastoral employments, and one of them, echoing the voice of all, says that " honest labour bears a lovely face." Not thus did the lot of the English peasant appear to Crabbe. He describes him toiling in summer "till the knees tremble and the temples beat"; in winter as "nipt by the frost and shivering in the wind," and thus hoarding up aches and weaknesses for old age, when the poorhouse receives him and all who share his poverty. Nothing escapes Crabbe's observation, and he seems to find most food for his art in scenes of flatness and desolation—trackless moors, slimy marshes, gloomy sea-coasts, with barren and unpicturesque cliffs—and portrays with evident pleasure the objects which tend to make a miserable scene still more miserable and desolate. The most inflexibly honest of poets, and one of the least ideal, he would never have praised the ethereal mildness of spring, when a bitter east wind was nipping the buds and blighting the apple blossoms. Fitzgerald, one of Tennyson's great friends, was a dear lover of Crabbe, and he relates how the Laureate once quoted from memory a fine passage from one of his tales, in which the autumn landscape seems to borrow its gloom from a conscience-stricken lover. I must tell you before reading the lines that the unfortunate young man, having made an offer

of marriage in a weak moment, which was
accepted much to his regret, retires for the
night "to think on what had past, to grieve
and to repent."

Early he rose and looked with many a sigh
On the red light that filled the eastern sky;
Oft had he stood before, alert and gay,
To hail the glories of the new-born day :
But now dejected, languid, listless, low,
He saw the wind upon the water blow,
And the cold stream curled onward as the gale
From the pine-hill blew harshly down the dale;
On the right side the youth a wood surveyed
With all its dark intensity of shade
When the rough wind alone was heard to move
In this the pause of nature and of love,
When now the young are reared, and when the old,
Lost to the tie, grow negligent and cold—
Far to the left he saw the huts of men,
Half hid in mist, that hung upon the fen ;
Before him swallows, gathering for the sea,
Took their short flights and twittered on the lea ;
And near the bean-sheaf stood, the harvest done,
And slowly blackened in the sickly sun ;
All these were sad in nature, or they took
Sadness from him, the likeness of his look,
And of his mind—he pondered for a while,
Then met his Fanny with a borrowed smile.

There is another fine scene of a like
character in Crabbe, in which Nature speaks
to an ardent lover in a voice of joy as he

hastens towards the loved one, and his visit being in vain, the prospect on the homeward journey loses all its beauty.

In the early morning with a joyous heart Orlando mounts his horse, and on passing over a desolate heath, exclaims :

This gay ling with all its purple flowers
A man at leisure might admire for hours,
This green-fringed cup-moss has a scarlet tip,
That yields to nothing but my Laura's lip;
And then how fine this herbage ! Man may say
A heath is barren, nothing is so gay.

He passes through lanes of burning sand and across a field where

Small black-legg'd sheep devour with hunger keen
The meagre herbage, fleshless, lank and lean.

Then a salt marsh charms Orlando and a stream that "rolls through its sloping banks of slimy mud."

Here on its wiry stem, in rigid bloom,
Grows the salt lavender that lacks perfume ;
Here the dwarf sallows creep, the sept-foil harsh,
And the soft slimy mallow of the marsh ;
Low on the ear the distant billows sound,
And just in view appears their stony bound ;
No hedge nor tree conceals the glowing sun,
Birds, save a wat'ry tribe, the district shun,
Nor chirp among the reeds where bitter waters run.
" Various as beautiful Nature is thy face,"
Exclaimed Orlando : all that grows has grace.

I

He reaches the beloved one's home only to receive a letter.

Gone to a friend, she tells me :—I commend
Her purpose means she to a female friend.

He resolves to follow his mistress to Loddon Hall, and the road passes through a lovely country, but all is changed for Orlando, and he finds no beauty in the fairest prospect.

I hate these long green lanes; there's nothing seen
In this vile country but eternal green;
Woods! waters! meadows! Will they never end?
'Tis a vile prospect :—Gone to see a friend!

You should read the brief biography of Crabbe written by his son, a highly attractive volume, and if you have read, or when you read, Jane Austen's novels, you will see how closely she resembled the poet in accuracy of observation, not indeed of nature, but of character, and you will under-stand perhaps what that dear lady meant when she said she could have married Crabbe.

Of the poets of our century Wordsworth stands in the very front rank, but the qualities which give him that position are

not such as youthful readers are likely
to appreciate. Wordsworth has not the
picturesque life and manly strength which
distinguish Scott; he has not the passion
any more than he has the morbidness of
Byron; he has not the enchanting music
of Coleridge or of Shelley. Sometimes, too,
he is terribly prosaic, and his want of
humour leads him to mistake childishness
for simplicity. There are lines in Wordsworth as bald and weak as any verses in
the language, and the writer was totally
unconscious of their poverty. His imagination does not create new worlds, but it
enables him to give a new life and meaning
to the world in which we live. He is at
once the humblest student of Nature and
the profoundest. Yet for Wordsworth
external nature has no deep significance
apart from humanity, and its "still, sad
music," to quote his own words, is heard
throughout his verse. But though pathetic
he is not melancholy, and his song, like all
noble poetry, inspires courage and faith.
Joy is the highest stimulant of the poetic
art, and Wordsworth, who called himself,
as I have already told you, one of the
happiest of men, when a sad hour comes,
as to all it will come, instead of desponding

sees the light beyond, and escaping quickly from the gloom, sings with the sun in his face. You will see this Wordsworthian characteristic in the *Ode on Immortality*, in *The Leech Gatherer*, in *The Happy Warrior*, in the *Lines composed above Tintern Abbey*, and in several of his lyrics and sonnets. I believe that in your best moments you will best appreciate Wordsworth. The more you feel the beauty of life and its serious-ness, the more will you find how much there is in his poetry to delight and to invigorate.

Matthew Arnold, who had studied his poetry with the seriousness of a disciple and the passion of a lover, has beautifully said of Wordsworth :—

> He found us when the age had bound
> Our souls in its benumbing round ;
> He spoke, and loosed our heart in tears,
> He laid us as we lay at birth
> On the cool flowery lap of earth,
> Smiles broke from us and we had ease ;
> The hills were round us, and the breeze
> Went o'er the sun-lit fields again ;
> Our foreheads felt the wind and rain,
> Our youth returned ; for there was shed
> On spirits that had long been dead,
> Spirits dried up and closely furled,
> The freshness of the early world.

He is indeed one of the wisest of poetical teachers, and a distinguished living poet, writing to me of Wordsworth and comparing him with Milton, says that he does not think him the least of the two. " If he is less lofty, he is deeper in thought and wider in the range of the humanities." For some time probably you must take much of Wordsworth's greatness on trust; yet if you have an ear and heart for poetry, you will surely feel a thrill of pleasure in reading the lines *To the Cuckoo, To a Highland Girl, To the Daisy, She was a Phantom of Delight, The Solitary Reaper, Yarrow Revisited*, and the lyric beginning " I wandered lonely." I think, too, you cannot fail to be struck by the classic dignity of *Laodamia*, and by that highly characteristic poem, *The Old Cumberland Beggar*. As you grow in years and knowledge, the more will you feel Wordsworth's power, and that his genius is equally at home in the highest theme and the humblest—in the *Ode to Duty*, and in such ballad-verses as *The Reverie of Poor Susan* and *We are Seven*. Sir Richard Steele, with a just appreciation of womanly goodness, said finely of Lady Elizabeth Hastings, that to know her was a liberal education. A similar praise may be awarded to Wordsworth. To use his own words, he gives us "nobler loves and nobler cares," and the purity and dignity of his verse exercise the same elevating influence of which we are conscious in the presence of a thoughtful and gracious Christian lady.

Several years ago, at a meeting of the "Wordsworth Society," Lord Selborne said :—

I speak no more and no less than the truth when I say that the acquaintance with the works of Wordsworth has been to me as great a power in the education of mind and character after the Bible as any that I have known. The Bible first, certainly. I think it has been to all who have given it a chance. Certainly it has been so to me. I put no book in competition with the Bible. But after the Bible, I trace more distinctly, with more certainty and with less hesitation and doubt, to Wordsworth, than to any other literary influence whatever, anything I may recognise as good in the formation of my own mind and character.

Lord Selborne's experience is that of many who have lived for a season with Wordsworth, have felt something of his joy, and gained solace from his wisdom.

Wordsworth held the theory that a poet

can utter what is in him in the ordinary
language of the common people.   In his
eagerness to escape from the ornate and
artificial diction of the poets of the eighteenth century, he strove, as Burns had
done before him without striving, to come
back to Nature by employing words which
might be used by any man or woman when
stirred by feeling.   His aim was praiseworthy, but the theory carried to an extreme
was untenable, and his effort therefore was
only partially successful.   You will see that
a reform was needed if I give you some
illustrations of the way in which the diction
of poetry had been corrupted in the century
which gave Wordsworth birth.

.   In the verse of Pope and in that of his
followers and successors every natural object
is described by a poetical equivalent.   The
moon is Cynthia, the sun Phœbus, the
nightingale Philomel ; a wood is a sylvan
shade, a girl a nymph, a shepherd a swain,
fishes the scaly breed ; and in singing of the
flowers of the field what better could a poet
of that age say than that "blushing Flora
paints the enamelled ground"? Mythological
allusions were also common, as indeed they
had been in a previous century, and the
gods and goddesses of Greece and Rome

walked in our city streets and in our woods and meadows. Pope cannot sing of *Windsor Forest* without introducing Neptune, Pan, and Diana, and by way of praising the beauty of the scene we are told that

> Not proud Olympus yields a nobler sight,
> Though gods assembled grace his towering height.

Even Gray, with his fine taste, sinned in this respect as much as Pope, or would have sinned as much if he had written as much. His odes abound with the diction that Wordsworth rejected with such contempt. He cannot call a spade a spade, and describes Eton boys chasing "the rolling circle's speed," which, in plain English, means trundling a hoop. He writes also of " rosy-bosomed hours," of " cool zephyr," and " fair Venus," and calls a cat a " hapless nymph " and a " presumptuous maid." Gray, you will see, had the taint of his age ; so had Thomson in a deadly degree, although he is one of the most original of descriptive poets, and gifted, to use a fine expression of his own, with " a great flame of imagination." Collins, too, who shares and more than shares with Gray the gift denied to his contemporaries of lyrical genius, was affected by the fashion of the time; and his friend, Thomas Warton the Laureate, although fortified by a love of natural beauty and of our early poets, goes astray from Nature while attempting to describe her. A rural poem of his, called *The Hermit*, is false in substance and artificial in expression. To assert that our farm-labourers "wish no beds of cygnet-down" or "trophied canopies" is nonsense, for how could they wish for luxuries or marks of wealth which they never saw, and of which they had never heard? Christopher Sly, of whom you will read in Shakespeare's *Comedy of Errors*, when put to bed in a nobleman's house and offered every kind of lordly comfort, did not cry out for wine, but for "a pot o' the smallest ale."

Now Wordsworth set his face like a flin against the conventional form of expression adopted by the poets popular in his youth. He asserts in an elaborate defence of his poetical creed that there neither is nor can be any essential difference between the language of prose and metrical composition, and that the metrical qualities needed to form a poet imply nothing differing in kind from other men, but only in degree. System, it has been said, is "the heavy lead of poetry," but Wordsworth, happily, on rising to the full height of his genius, flings his system to the winds, and while never using conventional terms, employs the language befitting a poet when lifted on the wings of imagination.

Before parting from Wordsworth, I must point out one striking characteristic of his poetry. There was a time in the earliest years of this century when England had to face Europe in arms, and was, as a great orator and preacher said, "most critically placed in the Thermopylæ of the universe." It was then that Wordsworth wrote poems —glowing with an emotion all the deeper, perhaps, since it was restrained within the limits of the sonnet—which testify that he also, as Milton had done before him, could make his voice sound like a trumpet. And listening to that voice, we feel that we may join the name of Wordsworth to that of the two mighty poets linked together in his verse.

> In our halls is hung
> Armoury of the invincible Knights of old :
> We must be free or die, who speak the tongue
> That Shakespeare spake ; the faith and morals hold
> Which Milton held.—In every thing we are sprung
> Of Earth's first blood, have titles manifold.

Thus also in 1802 did Wordsworth invoke the great poet of liberty :—

Milton ! thou should'st be living at this hour :
England hath need of thee : she is a fen
Of stagnant waters : altar, sword, and pen,
Fireside, the heroic wealth of hall and bower,
Have forfeited their ancient English dower
Of inward happiness.   We are selfish men ;
Oh ! raise us up, return to us again ;
And give us manners, virtue, freedom, power.
Thy soul was like a Star, and dwelt apart :
Thou hadst a voice whose sound was like the sea :
Pure as the naked heavens, majestic, free,
So didst thou travel on life's common way,
In cheerful godliness ; and yet thy heart
The lowliest duties on herself did lay.

In a sonnet written at Florence, Wordsworth relates how he was shown a seat that Dante had been accustomed to sit on. He gazed at it with awe, not venturing to occupy the marble stone that had been once so honoured, until he remembered that Dante was a patriot as well as a poet, and that he was a patriot also.

Bold with the thought in reverence I sate down,
And for a moment filled that empty Throne.

And here, let me observe that you will doubtless meet with persons who talk of patriotism as a narrow virtue or perhaps

as no virtue whatever. They will tell you
they are cosmopolitans, and that their love
embraces the whole world. Such language
has the sound of liberality, but it is a
foolish boast at best. The man who denies
that his own country is dearer to him than
a foreign land has probably but little love
for either. As reasonably might he say
that he loves the inhabitants of Central
Africa as much as his own children. If he
does, one pities the poor children. Weak
mortals such as we are have but limited
powers of intellect and affection. The
wider we can extend our love the better;
and Christianity teaches us, as no other
religion can, how to do this, but we must
begin by cherishing home affections. We
distrust the philanthropist who neglects his
own family; we distrust the statesman who
injures his country for the benefit of his
party; and we utterly distrust the Englishman whose expansive humanity leads him
to speak of England as he speaks of
Timbuctoo. Like all virtues, however,
patriotism must be tempered with dis-
cretion. In loving our own land, we must
allow for the love a foreigner feels for his,
and the true patriot will never love his
country so perversely as to sanction for

its sake injustice or aggression. Loving England well, he will love honour more.

> O ne'er enchained nor wholly vile,
> · O Albion, O my mother isle !

is the cry of Coleridge, whom Wordsworth called the most wonderful man he had ever met, and yet Wordsworth never duly estimated his poetry, which ranks with the most original and the most musical in the language. No poet has a more exquisite ear, and no poems are more unquestionably the work of poetical inspiration than the *Ancient Mariner* and *Christabel.* Coleridge is the poet of the supernatural; he is also the poet of the beautiful, and there are lines and stanzas in his verse not to be surpassed for charm.

In his highest moments, as in nearly all great poets, the sense of joy is paramount. Addressing a lady he says :—

> O Lady ! we receive but what we give,
> And in our life alone does Nature live:
> Ours is her wedding-garment, ours her shroud !
>
> .　　.　　.　　.　　.
>
> And from the soul itself must there be sent
> 　A sweet and potent voice, of its own birth,
> Of all sweet sounds the life and element !

O pure of heart! thou need'st not ask of me
What this strong music in the soul may be!
What, and wherein it doth exist,
This light, this glory, this fair luminous mist,
This beautiful and beauty-making power.
    Joy, virtuous Lady! Joy that ne'er was given,
Save to the pure, and in their purest hour,
Life, and Life's effluence, cloud at once and shower,
Joy, Lady! is the spirit and the power,
Which wedding Nature to us gives in dower,
    A new Earth and new Heaven,
Undreamt of by the sensual and the proud—
Joy is the sweet voice, Joy the luminous cloud—
    We in ourselves rejoice!
And thence flows all that charms or ear or sight,
    All melodies the echoes of that voice,
All colours a suffusion from that light.

In Wordsworth's great ode on *Intimations of Immortality* there is the same belief that all true life is rooted in joy. What although age, he exclaims, takes away the glory and the dream of youth; do we not gain a deeper blessedness in place of those fugitive pleasures?

What though the radiance which was once so bright
Be now for ever taken from my sight,
    Though nothing can bring back the hour
Of splendour in the grass, of glory in the flower;
    We will grieve not, rather find
    Strength in what remains behind;
    In the primal sympathy
    Which having been must ever be;

In the soothing thoughts that spring
Out of human suffering;
In the faith that looks through death,
In years that bring the philosophic mind.

And O, ye Fountains, Meadows, Hills, and Groves,
Forebode not any severing of our loves !
Yet in my heart of hearts I feel your might ;
I only have relinquished one delight
To live beneath your more habitual sway.
I love the Brooks which down their channels fret,
Even more than when I tripped lightly as they ;
The innocent brightness of a new-born Day
Is lovely yet ;
The Clouds that gather round the setting sun
Do take a sober colouring from an eye
That hath kept watch o'er man's mortality ;
Another race hath been, and other palms are won.
Thanks to the human heart by which we live,
Thanks to its tenderness, its joys, and fears,
To me the meanest flower that blows can give
Thoughts that do often lie too deep for tears.

It is strange to remember that Coleridge's loveliest poetry was written within the short period of five or six years; still stranger to think how small in bulk is the treasure left by this distinguished poet. When you have read the two poems already mentioned, *The Three Graves; France : an Ode;* the *Hymn in the Vale of Chamouni, Work without Hope, The Garden of Boc-*

caccio, *Kubla Khan*, *Love*, *Dejection*, and *Youth and Age*, you will, I think, have read all the verse of Coleridge that is of prime excellence.   Other poems there are we should be greatly sorry to lose, but those I have mentioned belong to that rare order of poetry on which Time will lay his hand in vain.

Coleridge lived to face the approaches of old age.   He was indeed an old man before his time.   John Keats died at twenty-six, but these poets, who had no more personal knowledge of each other than could be gained from a hand-shake,[1] had this in common — a rapturous sense of beauty, an ear for rare harmonies, an imagination that carried them into far-off regions of romance, where

> Magic casements open on the foam
> Of perilous seas in faery lands forlorn.

---

[1] They met in a lane between Hampstead and Highgate, and Coleridge's ominous remark to his companion when they parted was, " There is death in that hand."   Keats had more to say of the poet whose reputation had been long established :—
" I walked with him at his alderman-after-dinner pace for near two miles, I suppose.   In those two miles he broached a thousand things. . . . I heard his voice as he came towards me—I heard it as he moved away—I had heard it all the interval—if it may be called so.   He was civil enough to ask me to call on him at Highgate."   Keats did not go, and the two poets never met again.

And—

> Where Alph, the sacred river, ran
> Through caverns measureless to man
> Down to a sunless sea.

It is rare indeed that genius descends from parent to child, but Samuel Taylor Coleridge had a son named Hartley who was as true, though very far from being as great a poet as his father. It has been said that he led a wasted life. I do not know, but there was much in it to be sorrowed over. It is something to be loved as he was, and his bitter experience was not without fruit in his verse. When you read his sad story and his beautiful sonnets, as some day you must, you will like to think of the erring but not ignoble poet who, when his head was gray, was "nor child, nor man, nor youth, nor sage," lying by the side of his illustrious friend and affectionate counsellor, Wordsworth, in Grasmere Churchyard. What poet could have a sweeter resting-place! Here is a little song from his pen which any poet would be proud to have written :—

> She is not fair to outward view
> As many maidens be,

K

Her loveliness I never knew
  Until she smiled on me;
Oh! then I saw her eye was bright,
A well of love, a spring of light!

But now her looks are coy and cold,
  To mine they ne'er reply,
And yet I cease not to behold
  The love-light in her eye;
Her very frowns are fairer far
Than smiles of other maidens are!

Walter Savage Landor, a fine poet, but far better known by his prose writings, called Wordsworth, Coleridge, and Southey three towers of one castle. If I were to talk to you freely of these famous men, I should perhaps tire you, so very much there is to say about them. Southey, though he had a great gift of invention and much poetical energy, has no claim, as a poet, to be ranked with his two friends. He has written a few beautiful poems and some imperishable prose—I hope you have read his *Life of Nelson*—but his moral character and his splendid courage as a man of letters are more impressive than his poetry, and I do not think Sir Henry Taylor is wrong in his judgment, that, take Southey for all in all, "it may be said of him justly, and with no straining of the truth, that of all his contemporaries he was the greatest MAN."

" Much have I travelled in the realms of gold," said Keats, and the fruit he gleaned from his travels is of the richest flavour. Keats is one of the most poetical of poets. He lived for poetry. It was his supreme joy, his hope, his work, his constant thought. On this his ambition was centred, and young though he was, there are indications that he took a just estimate of his power. What you will chiefly observe in his earliest poems is a luxuriance of imagery and a want of the restraint a poet owes to art. In the later poems there is also a lavish wealth of imagery, but it is combined with a perfect mastery of form and an incomparable power in the use of words. Indeed, I do not know anything more remarkable than the way in which, as a poet, Keats sprang from boyhood to full maturity in a space of little more than two years. In his character there were some defects which seemed to be lessening before he died; in his verse, the over-sensuousness and laxity of style that mark *Endymion* were quickly exchanged for the calm beauty of *Hyperion*, and for the lovely art of such poems as *The Eve of St. Agnes*, the odes *To Autumn*,

To a Nightingale, and *To a Grecian Urn.*
Of the odes the most perfect perhaps, for I
do not venture to speak with certainty, is
the address *To Autumn,* and this therefore
I will read to you.

Season of mists and mellow fruitfulness,
　　Close bosom-friend of the maturing sun;
Conspiring with him how to load and bless
　　With fruit the vines that round the thatch-eaves run;
To bend with apples the moss'd cottage-trees,
　　And fill all fruit with ripeness to the core;
　　　　To swell the gourd, and plump the hazel shells
With a sweet kernel; to set budding more,
　　And still more, later flowers for the bees,
　　Until they think warm days will never cease,
　　　　For Summer has o'er-brimm'd their clammy cells.

Who hath not seen thee oft amid thy store?
　　Sometimes whoever seeks abroad may find
Thee sitting careless on a granary floor,
　　Thy hair soft-lifted by the winnowing wind;
Or on a half-reap'd furrow sound asleep,
　　Drows'd with the fume of poppies, while thy hook
　　　　Spares the next swath and all its twined flowers:
And sometimes like a gleaner thou dost keep
　　Steady thy laden head across a brook;
　　Or by a cyder-press, with patient look,
　　　　Thou watchest the last oozings hours by hours.

Where are the songs of Spring? Ay, where are they?
　　Think not of them, thou hast thy music too,—

While barred clouds bloom the soft-dying day,
  And touch the stubble-plains with rosy hue;
Then in a wailful choir the small gnats mourn
  Among the river sallows, borne aloft
    Or sinking as the light wind lives or dies;
And full-grown lambs loud bleat from hilly bourn;
  Hedge-crickets sing; and now with treble soft
  The red-breast whistles from a garden-croft;
    And gathering swallows twitter in the skies.

" No one else," says Mr. Matthew Arnold,
" in English poetry, save Shakespeare, has
in expression quite the fascinating felicity
of Keats, his perfection of loveliness."
Read *The Eve of St. Agnes*, and you will
understand something of the genius which
gives to Keats a place among the great poets.
Read *Hyperion*, and you will see how, despite his love of luxuriant imagery, he was
able to curb all extravagances of language
and fancy, and to rise into the serene
region of the epic poet. This is not all.
The sonnet is a difficult form of composition,
for the aim of the poet is to express within
its narrow bounds one nobly imaginative
thought. This difficulty has been overcome
by Keats, and his early sonnet—*On First
Looking into Chapman's Homer*—ranks with
the best in our literature. As I owe to it
a beautiful title for these " Talks," it is im-

possible to speak of Keats without reading
it to you :—

> Much have I travell'd in the realms of gold,
>   And many goodly states and kingdoms seen ;
>   Round many western islands have I been
> Which bards in fealty to Apollo hold.
> Oft of one wide expanse had I been told
>   That deep-brow'd Homer ruled as his demesne ;
>   Yet did I never breathe its pure serene
> Till I heard Chapman speak out loud and bold :
> Then felt I like some watcher of the skies
>   When a new planet swims into his ken ;
> Or like stout Cortez when with eagle eyes
>   He star'd at the Pacific—and all his men
> Look'd at each other with a wild surmise—
>   Silent, upon a peak in Darien.

To Keats the charm of Chapman's
version of Homer was probably found in
the translator's gift of coining poetical
phrases, and in the "long-resounding march"
of his metre, which consists of fourteen
syllables. George Chapman was one of
the Elizabethans, and I will give you a
brief specimen of the way in which he
represented Homer.

> The youths crowned cups of wine,
> Drank off, and filled again to all : that day was held
>   divine

And spent in Pæans to the sun; who heard with
    pleased ear;
When whose bright chariot stooped to sea, and
    twilight hid the clear,
All soundly on their cables slept, even till the night
    was won;
And when the Lady of the Light, the rosy-fingered
    morn,
Rose from the hills; all fresh arose and to the camp
    retired,
Apollo with a foreright-wind their swelling bark
    inspired.

Like so many poets, Keats, with the
intensest faculty for enjoyment, had also
much to suffer. He was very young, and
inspired alike by love and poetry, when the
fine gold of his life was suddenly dimmed
by signs not to be mistaken of the approach
of consumption. He was born for early
death, and haunted by a great fear and a
great love he said that his heart was broken.
Severn, a well-known artist, and the most
faithful of friends, watched over him day by
day in Rome and saw the gradual but sure
extinction of the faint hopes which the poet
still cherished. He felt, he said, the flowers
growing over him, and there were moments
when he longed to put an end to his misery.

In religion (says his biographer, Mr. Colvin),

Keats had been neither a believer nor a scoffer, respecting Christianity without calling himself a Christian, and by turns clinging to and drifting from the doctrine of immortality. Contrasting now the behaviour of the believer Severn with his own, he acknowledged anew the power of the Christian teaching and example, and bidding Severn read to him from Jeremy Taylor's *Holy Living and Dying*, strove to pass the remainder of his days in a temper of more peace and constancy.

The whole story of his love and of his poetry is infinitely pathetic, and that a poet who died at the early age of twenty-six should have left such an inestimable legacy to his country, tells us how rich may be the life confined within a narrow space.

> Circles are praised, not that abound
> In largeness, but th' exactly round ;
> So life we praise that does excel
> Not in much time but acting well.

" A thing of beauty is a joy for ever," and that is the joy Keats has left us. Since the days of Spenser there has been perhaps no poet whose song is dedicated to beauty with a devotion so entire.

Shelley has been described as " a beautiful and ineffectual angel beating in the void his luminous wings in vain." He has wings if ever poet had, and seldom rests upon the earth at all. Unlike Wordsworth's skylark, it cannot be said of Shelley that he is true to the kindred points of heaven and home; rather, like his own skylark, he is a scorner of the ground, and from the cloud-land in which he loves best to dwell "showers a rain of melody."

So much passionate nonsense has been written about Shelley, that there is a danger lest, in the love of truth and in the exercise of common sense, we should be tempted to depreciate his genius. This, however, will be impossible if we are familiar—as every student of poetry ought to be—with his lyrics, in which the singer's voice attains an altitude that has been rarely if ever surpassed in English song. The little volume of poems from Shelley selected by Mr. Stopford Brooke will introduce you to the finest gold of his genius. Read the love lyrics, *Epipsychidion*, *The Sensitive Plant*, *Ode to the West Wind*, and the pieces which Mr. Brooke has classed under *Poems of Nature and Man*, and you will be able to form some idea of this poet's art. Shelley is among the saddest of poets, and in one of his poems, written in dejection, he says:—

Alas! I have nor hope nor health,
Nor peace within, nor calm around,
Nor that content, surpassing wealth,
The sage in meditation found,
And walked with inward glory crowned—
Nor fame, nor power, nor love, nor leisure.

And then he adds that he could lie down like a tired child and weep away his life of care. But Shelley knew, as Coleridge knew, that the best nutriment of song is joy, and that "thence flows all that charms or ear or sight," and one of his loveliest lyrics is an invocation to the Spirit of Delight :—

Rarely, rarely, comest thou,
  Spirit of Delight,
Wherefore hast thou left me now
  Many a day and night?
Many a weary night and day
'Tis since thou art fled away.

.   .   .   .

I love all that thou lovest,
  Spirit of Delight!
The fresh Earth in new leaves drest
  And the starry night;
Autumn evening, and the morn
When the golden mists are born.

.   .   .   .   .   .

I love Love, though he has wings,
  And like light can flee,
But above all other things,
  Spirit, I love thee—

Thou art love and life! O come,
Make once more my heart thy home.

Sixty or seventy years ago Lord Byron was by far the most popular poet in England. It is difficult now to understand how with such poets before them as Wordsworth, Coleridge, and Shelley, some critical students of poetry preferred Byron; but much of the preference was due to his extraordinary personality. He wrote in energetic verse of his private affairs, and people who loved scandal or sympathised with an emotion much of which we now know to be unreal, liked to read it. He was a nobleman of striking beauty, and a poet of extraordinary though ill-regulated genius. His eccentricities and excesses were the talk of society, and people who ought to have known better excused his vices on the plea that he was too great a genius to be bound by ordinary rules. Much of his poetry rings hollow, and far from being genuine metal is little better than pinchbeck. On the other hand, there is much that shows a sincere though often morbid love of Nature, and in his best work an energy, reminding us of Dryden, carries the reader along with a force to which he is compelled to yield.

I cannot believe that Byron will be ever

again a popular poet, nor do I understand how Matthew Arnold, who loved Wordsworth so well, could place Byron by his side, and call the two a glorious pair "pre-eminent in actual performance among the English poets of this century." Byron's immorality, which is that of the mocker who has no respect for virtue, is against him in the race for fame, but there are also distinctly literary and poetical qualities in which his work is deficient. In style he is slovenly, and for the finer harmonies of verse he has no ear whatever; his subject-matter is frequently meretricious, and his egotism sickly. He had indeed great qualities, but they are rather those of the wit and satirist than of the imaginative poet, and unfortunately these powers are so wantonly exercised that Byron sometimes spoils his finest work. It may be possible, I know, to point to poems in the large mass of his poetry that will contradict this estimate,—lovely oases in a spacious desert, but I venture to think that I am right in the main.

I shall not be surprised, however, if some young readers disagree with me. Byron's verse, though not musical, is forcible, and poems or stanzas easy to learn by heart and of incontestable merit are to be found in all selections.   If you admire such pieces as *The Isles of Greece*, the Stanzas to his Sister, the Address to the Ocean, the brilliant picture of the night before Waterloo at Brussels, *The Prisoner of Chillon*, the opening lines of *The Corsair*, the lines on Death, and the two stanzas on Solitude, it is not for me to say your taste is false, for I learnt all these passages in boyhood, and can repeat them and enjoy them still.

And now I want to draw your attention to a poet who was a young woman of twenty-five when Lord Byron died, and with her passionate enthusiasm for the poetic art felt what Matthew Arnold expressed years afterwards :—

> When Byron's eyes were shut in death,
> We bow'd our head and held our breath.
> He taught us little ; but our soul
> Had felt him like the thunder's roll.
> With shivering heart the strife we saw
> Of Passion with Eternal Law ;
> And yet with reverential awe
> We watch'd the fount of fiery life
> Which served for that Titanic strife.

Elizabeth Barrett, who became the wife of the profound thinker and poet who now rests among his peers in Westminster

Abbey, was a verse-maker from her childhood, and in early womanhood was distinguished by her acquirements. She read Greek with ease, and translated the *Prometheus Bound* of Æschylus, yet the sanity and moderation of Greek poetry do not seem to have influenced her own productions. She is probably the greatest female poet, not of England only, but of Europe—assuredly the greatest and sweetest we possess, unless, indeed, Christina Rossetti shares the throne with her. If Mrs. Browning's taste and judgment had been equal to her inspiration, her place would have been with the first poets of her country. Unfortunately her passionate enthusiasm, her sensibility, and fancy are exercised without the self-restraint which should guide the pen of the artist. "An author," said Dryden, "is not to write all he can, but only all he ought." Mrs. Browning, like Dryden himself, too often forgot this wise rule, and in the midst of verses perfect in simplicity and beauty the reader lights upon stanzas that make him shiver. She turns adjectives into nouns, coins words that are false to the idiom of the language, and forgets that grammar has some claims even upon poets.

But in this talk about great poets I want to call forth your admiration, and not to dwell upon defects. There is a time for criticism, but it must be based upon love, and the more you read of Mrs. Browning's poetry, the warmer, I think, that love will grow. Like a true woman, she puts her heart into her verse, and her loveliest poetry is due to personal feeling. The little we know of the story of her life adds an interest to her poetry. We think of the enthusiastic girl in early life gathering knowledge from all sources and in all languages. Books were her world; and what a happy world it is! Slight in figure, "with a shower of dark curls falling on each side of a most expressive face, large, tender eyes, richly fringed by dark eyelashes, and a smile like a sunbeam"—how pleasant a picture is this of the young scholar and poet! Possibly her mind had been overtasked by long years of study, for at the age of twenty-eight she broke a blood-vessel in the lungs. Two years later, while trying to recover health at Torquay, a brother whom she much loved was drowned in her sight; and from that moment the poet's health seemed to break down utterly. But love, which is stronger than death, came to her rescue;

and how love saved her she describes in
those wonderful sonnets in which, under
the pretence of a translation from the
Portuguese, she addressed her lover and
husband.

> Then love me, Love! look on me . . . breathe on
> me!
> As brighter ladies do not count it strange,
> For love to give up acres and degree,
> I yield the grave for thy sake, and exchange
> My near sweet view of Heaven, for earth with Thee.

And so the invalid, strong in hope and
joy, was carried away from England to
dwell under the sunnier sky of Italy.   There
her boy was born, and some happy years
of wedded life were spent in Florence,
where she lived long enough to witness
the independence of a country she dearly
loved, and to which much of her verse is
dedicated.

It is often the case that a poet's fame
rests upon short poems.   It is so with Gray
and Collins, with Burns and Campbell, and
although *Aurora Leigh*, a poem containing
twelve thousand lines, has some irregular
bursts of poetry which Mrs. Browning has
never surpassed, I think you will gain, as
I have done, the greatest delight from her
lyrics and sonnets.   Seldom has she written

a flawless poem, but she has written many in which the beauty is so exquisite that its faults are comparatively unheeded. Such, for example, are the *Rhyme of the Duchess May*, *The Cry of the Children*, *The Deserted Garden*, *My Doves*, *Sleeping and Watching*, *A Sabbath Morning at Sea*, *Cowper's Grave*, *A Child's Grave at Florence*, *The Swan's Nest*, *The Sleep*, and that remarkable though far from perfect poem, *Lady Geraldine's Courtship*. Now if you read these lyrical poems, and enter into the spirit of them, you will find yourself in a new world of poetry—a world that owes its existence to Mrs. Browning's genius. An accomplished versifier may give you pleasure if he has some charm of fancy and expression, but he cannot carry his readers into a realm which is at once strange and beautiful, for that is the supreme gift of the poet. Many a graceful poem is written in these days, which we read, like, and forget in a week, but a true poet will not allow you to forget him so readily. His strength of imagination holds you captive as the Wedding Guest in Coleridge's poem was held by the Ancient Mariner, so that you cannot choose but hear. It is a great thing to have a voice ; the poetaster has only an echo.

L

In this respect, but in no other, Thomas Hood resembles Mrs. Browning. He is a minor poet, but a true one, and a true humorist also, although forced, unluckily, to make fun for his daily bread. I think you will like his serious poems, and some especially in which humour is blended with pathos. If ever man loved the art, Thomas Hood did, and among the singers of the century I may venture to say he must always hold a place. If you ask me my reason for so confident an assertion, I reply that Hood has in his best poems great perfection of workmanship, the simplicity that instinctively avoids what is meretricious, much poetical sensibility, and sufficient imagination to see with perfect clearness the object he describes. There is art as well as the deepest pathos in *The Bridge of Sighs*, and to have written a poem like this and a poem like *The Song of the Shirt* is to have done far more probably for the good of his kind than many a man has done whose charity strikes the world more forcibly. Do not suppose, as some benevolent people do, that all Christian work must be done in one direction. It is good to distribute tracts and blankets, good, as St. James says, to visit the fatherless, good to praise and pray, but it is also good to write poetry, for that is to exercise one of the noblest of gifts, and, as George Herbert says—

> Λ verse may find him who a sermon flies
> And turn delight into a sacrifice.

FIFTH TALK

In speaking to you of the poets of our century you will have observed that only casual mention has been made of Sir Walter Scott. He was, as you know, the contemporary and friend of Wordsworth, and if a regard were paid to chronology, should have come next to him in this survey. But upon you as youthful students and readers, Scott has larger claims than any other author of the age, and I have therefore thought it would interest you to speak of him more freely, and to devote an hour this evening to the consideration of his works.

The name of Sir Walter Scott is one of the greatest in literature, and, which is better still, one of the purest. In all that he wrote, whether in verse or prose, there is a wholesome and invigorating power. George Eliot speaks of Sir Walter as that "beloved writer who has made a chief part in the happiness of many young lives";

but I believe that readers who found Scott a delight in youth love him also in old age. Scott is in the nineteenth century what Shakespeare was in the sixteenth. Both are brothers in creative genius, in largeness of sympathy, in freedom from self-consciousness, in the love of Nature, in their appreciation of the humours of life, and in a sense of its pathos. Do not suppose that I am comparing these two great men in point of genius, but there are many respects in which Sir Walter Scott comes nearer to Shakespeare than any other imaginative writer.

It is the fashion of some critics to depreciate his genius as a poet, chiefly because his verse is unlike that most in vogue nowadays. If his poetry were hard to understand and needed commentators, it would probably be more admired. And in judging of a poet it is folly to look for qualities that he does not possess. Scott's forte is that of the ballad-writer, and he has the ballad-writer's carelessness and dash; he has also the ballad-writer's spirit and more than one splendid gift that belongs to himself alone. There are passages in his verse which of the kind are unequalled in modern literature. When Scott began his poetical career, there was much false taste in fashion and a craving after the sentimentality to which, in Sir Walter's babyhood, Goethe, the greatest of German poets, gave vitality by his *Sorrows of Werther*. John Wesley, on casually taking up Sterne's *Sentimental Journey*, exclaimed, " *Senti-mental*, what is that? It is not English. He might as well say *continental*. It is not sense. It conveys no determinate idea, yet one fool makes many. And this nonsensical word—who would believe it? —is become a fashionable one!" The word was apparently coined at this period, for it is not in the early editions of Johnson's Dictionary; but what we understand by sentimentality—an extravagant and un-healthy excess of feeling—was rampant during the most susceptible period of Scott's life. He had not a touch of it himself. In one of his letters he says that he has "a most unsentimental horror for sentimental letters," and the complaint in any form was distasteful to this manly poet.

His love of Nature and of song was stimulated by what in some respects proved a lifelong misfortune. An infantile com-plaint made the child lame, and he was sent from Edinburgh to a farmhouse in the country.

When the day was fine (he writes) I was usually carried out and laid down beside an old shepherd among the crags and rocks round which he fed his sheep. Here I delighted to roll about all day long in the midst of the flock, and "the sort of fellowship I thus formed with the sheep and lambs impressed my mind with a degree of affectionate feeling towards them which lasted throughout life." The impatience of a child soon inclined me to struggle with my infirmity, and I began by degrees to stand, to walk, and to run.

The happiness of these baby days at Sandy-Knowe is recalled in some beautiful lines in the introduction to the third canto of *Marmion*. After saying that poetic impulse was given "by the green hill and clear blue heaven," the poet adds :—

> It was a barren scene, and wild,
> Where naked cliffs were rudely piled ;
> But ever and anon between
> Lay velvet tufts of loveliest green ;
> And well the lonely infant knew
> Recesses where the wall-flower grew,
> And honeysuckle loved to crawl
> Up the low crag and ruin'd wall.

I deem'd such nooks the sweetest shade
The sun in all its round survey'd.

There the child not only gained a love of Nature, but of the ballads recited by the country people. Even in early boyhood he read immensely and forgot nothing. Gradually he became strong and was sent to school, where, despite his lameness, he showed great physical energy, and also gained his first laurels as a story-teller. At thirteen, while staying with his aunt at Kelso, a place very dear to him in later years, not only for its beauty, but from these youthful memories, he became acquainted with Percy's *Reliques of Ancient Poetry*, and from that hour ballad poetry had for Scott an irresistible fascination.

I remember well (he says) the spot where I read these volumes for the first time. It was beneath a huge platanus-tree, in the ruins of what had been intended for an old-fashioned arbour in the garden. The summer day sped onward so fast, that notwithstanding the sharp appetite of thirteen, I forgot the hour of dinner, was sought for with anxiety, and was still found entranced in my intellectual banquet. To read and to remember was in this instance the same thing, and henceforth I overwhelmed my school-fellows, and all who would hearken to me, with tragical recitations from the ballads of Bishop Percy. The first time, too, I could scrape a few shillings together, which were not common occurrences with me, I bought unto myself a copy of these beloved volumes : nor do I believe I ever read a book half so frequently, or with half the enthusiasm. . . . To this period also I can trace distinctly the awaking of that delightful feeling for the beauties of natural objects which has never since deserted me.

I am not going to take you step by step over the familiar ground covered by Scott's poetry, for I trust I am not mistaken in supposing that to all of you it is familiar. On some of its characteristics, however, it may be well that a few words should be said. His earliest efforts were as a translator of German ballads, and ere long some original ballads from his pen exhibited the energy and fervour that mark his most spirited verses. The following stanzas were sufficient to announce the advent of a true poet:—

Through the huge oaks of Evandale,
  Whose limbs a thousand years have worn,
What sullen roar comes down the gale,
  And drowns the hunter's pealing horn?

Mightiest of all the beasts of chase,
That roam in woody Caledon,
Crashing the forest in his race,
The Mountain Bull comes thundering on.

Fierce, on the hunter's quiver'd band,
He rolls his eyes of swarthy glow,
Spurns with black hoof and horn the sand,
And tosses high his mane of snow.

The poet Campbell relates how he was wont to recite these lines on the North Bridge of Edinburgh, so that the whole fraternity of coachmen knew him by tongue as he passed, and it is characteristic of Scott's vigorous poetry, that it haunts the memory, and tempts the reader to shout its trumpet-like notes aloud.

The publication of *The Lay of the Last Minstrel* was received with unbounded applause, for, despite some obvious faults, its fire and originality took many a heart by storm. In it Scott struck for the first time the note of patriotism which distinguishes him as it does Shakespeare, Sir Walter's great contemporary Wordsworth, and indeed every poet worthy of the name. Who is there that does not remember the splendid passage in which the minstrel invokes a poetical curse upon the man

With soul so dead
Who never to himself has said,
This is my own, my native land,
Whose heart hath ne'er within him burned
As home his footsteps he has turned
From wandering on a foreign strand.

Three years later *Marmion*, his finest poem, was welcomed with even greater enthusiasm than the *Lay*.

In his magnificent picture of the battle-field at Flodden, Scott rises to a height he never reached before or after. So far as my knowledge goes, there is nothing of the kind finer in literature than the death of Marmion, and listen to me as I read the vigorous description with which the defeat of Scotland closes :—

But as they left the dark'ning heath,
More desperate grew the strife of death.
The English shafts in volleys hail'd,
In headlong charge their horse assail'd ;
Front, flank, and rear, the squadrons sweep
To break the Scottish circle deep,
    That fought around their King.
But yet, though thick the shafts as snow,
Though charging knights like whirlwinds go,
Though bill-men ply the ghastly blow,
    Unbroken was the ring ;
The stubborn spear-men still made good
Their dark impenetrable wood,

Each stepping where his comrade stood,
The instant that he fell.
No thought was there of dastard flight;—
Link'd in the serried phalanx tight,
Groom fought like noble, squire like knight,
As fearlessly and well;
Till utter darkness closed her wing
O'er their thin host and wounded King.
Then skilful Surrey's sage commands
Led back from strife his shatter'd bands;
And from the charge they drew,
As mountain-waves, from wasted lands,
Sweep back to ocean blue.
Then did their loss his foemen know;
Their King, their Lords, their mightiest low,
They melted from the field, as snow,
When streams are swoln and south winds blow,
Dissolves in silent dew.
Tweed's echoes heard the ceaseless plash,
While many a broken band,
Disorder'd, through her currents dash,
To gain the Scottish land;
To town and tower, to down and dale,
To tell red Flodden's dismal tale,
And raise the universal wail.
Tradition, legend, tune, and song,
Shall many an age that wail prolong:
Still from the sire the son shall hear
Of the stern strife, and carnage drear,
Of Flodden's fatal field,
Where shiver'd was fair Scotland's spear,
And broken was her shield!

Even *Marmion* had to yield in popularity to *The Lady of the Lake*, which created a *furore* for Scottish travel, and made the Highlands as familiar as they had been previously dreaded or despised. Scott was now, as Lord Byron called him, the " Monarch of Parnassus," but he cared nothing for popular applause and never showed the slightest trace of literary vanity. He always underestimated his gifts as a poet. When his little girl Sophia was asked how she liked *The Lady of the Lake*, she replied, "Oh, I have not read it; papa says there is nothing so bad for young people as reading bad poetry." One day his eldest boy came home from the High School at Edinburgh with blood upon his face. He had been called " The Lady of the Lake," and having never heard of the poem, had objected to being called a lassie, and had fought in defence of his manliness.

The poem has much in it that is very charming, especially in the descriptive passages, but it is too much of a story in verse, and in poetry the interest of the tale should not predominate.

As a lyric poet Sir Walter has genuine power. In addition to his spirited ballads, he has written many a lovely song full of tenderness and pathos. Using the simplest words, he produces the most striking effect. Some of these lyrics are to be found in the narrative poems, and many of the most charming are scattered through the *Waverley Novels*, and gain additional beauty from their appropriateness to the circumstances and characters of the story.

So heartily do I love Scott, that I should like to say to you, Read all the poetry he has written, but if you have not leisure to do this, you ought at least to have an intimate knowledge of the poems I have mentioned, and can leave for a more convenient season *Rokeby*, *The Lord of the Isles*, and *The Bridal of Triermain*. I may add that the more you know of Sir Walter's noble character, the more will his works be appreciated, and that to his admirers there is not one of his romances so attractive as his Journal, and Lockhart's fascinating biography.

And now I shall try and tell you, though it must needs be very imperfectly, what I think and what I hope you will learn to think of those great works the *Waverley Novels*, for great they are in imagination, in humour, in variety of knowledge, in reverence for what is noble, in breadth of toleration, and in the charm inspired by poetic feeling.

It is one of the first requisites of the novelist that he should have a good story to tell and know how to tell it, and in this respect there are several masterpieces among the *Waverley Novels*. Nothing can be more admirable than the choice of subject and the management of the plot in *Old Mortality, The Bride of Lammermoor, The Fortunes of Nigel, Quentin Durward, Kenilworth*, and I might add, *The Heart of Midlothian*, were it not that Scott has somewhat injured this splendid fiction by prolonging the story after the interest is over. Another prominent mark of these tales is their wonderful variety, their richness in incident and life. The reader becomes acquainted with public men and public affairs, with the homeliest domestic details, and the humblest people. He is brought into the company of kings and queens, of beggars and clowns, of mercenary soldiers and chivalrous gentlemen, of eccentric wits and humorous pedants, of magistrates and lawyers, of servant-girls and high-born ladies ; and whether the plot is laid in the twelfth century, as in *Ivanhoe*, or in the eighteenth, as in *Guy Mannering* and *The Antiquary*, there is the one touch of Nature which makes the reader feel as if all these people were something more than creatures of the imagination, and must have played their parts on the stage of life. Naturally Scott is most at home on his native soil, and in picturing scenes and people familiar to him all his life. Yet I think there is as much truth to nature and to history in the wonderful portraits of Louis XI. and Charles the Bold in *Quentin Durward*, of King James in *The Fortunes of Nigel*, and of Mary Queen of Scots in *The Abbot*, as in the characters which he may be said to have drawn from living persons. We cannot say, of course, that the historical personages that figure in Scott's pages talked as he makes them talk, but the reader feels sure that if they did not, they ought to have done so. And the homelier folk, like Maggie Mucklebackit in *The Antiquary*, or Meg Dods in *St. Ronan's Well*, or Dandie Dinmont in *Guy Mannering*, are to the reader as much alive as if they were in the flesh.

Probably, as readers not yet old enough to be critical, you care much less for vivid portraiture of character than for exciting incident, and of this there is assuredly no lack in the *Waverley Novels*. Turn, for instance, to the description in *The Legend of Montrose* of Dalgetty in the dungeon ; to the interview between Morton and Burley in the cave, which you will find in *Old Mortality;* to the midnight murder of the miser Trapbois in *The Fortunes of Nigel;* to the trial by combat in *The Fair Maid of Perth;* to the picture of Jeanie Deans in the barn with ruffians; to the startling scenes with De La Marck in *Quentin Durward;* to Rob Roy's escape from his captors in the novel named after that hero; and to such novels as *Ivanhoe, The Talisman, Kenilworth,* and *Guy Mannering,* which abound in the most spirit-stirring actions. This, indeed, is a characteristic of the novels throughout.

In July 1814 *Waverley,* the first of the romances, appeared in three volumes. The excitement and interest created by this tale cannot easily be exaggerated. It opened up a new world; and Goethe, the great poet of Germany, said it might be placed beside the best works that have ever been written. He thought Scott never surpassed or even equalled it, but this is not the general opinion; and, indeed, such is the versatility of his genius as a romance-writer, that it is seldom that readers who talk together over the novels agree in preferring the same tale. Wonderful was the rapidity with which a part of the story was written, the second

M

and third volumes having been composed between 4th June and 1st July, during which time Scott was in Edinburgh attending to his official duties for some hours daily.

Lockhart, Scott's future son-in-law and biographer, was in Edinburgh at the time, and on dining one evening with some young men in a house at right angles with Scott's residence in Castle Street, he relates that, upon seeing his youthful host look uncomfortable, he asked if he were unwell.

" No," said he, " I shall be well enough presently, if you will only let me sit where you are and take my chair, for there is a confounded hand in sight of me here which has often bothered me before, and now it won't let me fill my glass with a good will." I rose to change places with him accordingly, and he pointed out to me this hand which, like the writing on Belshazzar's wall, disturbed his hour of hilarity. " Since we sat down," he said, " I have been watching it ; it fascinates my eye—it never stops —page after page is finished and thrown on that heap of MS., and still it goes on unwearied —and so it will be till candles are brought in, and God knows how long after that. It is the same every night—I can't stand the sight of it when I'm not at my books." " Some stupid, dogged, engrossing clerk probably," exclaimed myself or some other giddy youth in our society. "No, boys," said our host, "I well know what hand it is—'tis Sir Walter Scott's."

This rapidity led Carlyle to say in one of the least worthy efforts of his pen, that "no great thing was ever or will ever be done with ease but with difficulty."

The remark is a just one, but in applying it as he does to Scott it will not bear examination. The greatest of romance-writers was more than forty years of age before he wrote his first tale. Throughout his life he had been laying up the stores which his wonderful genius enabled him afterwards to use so freely. He came to the work with a full mind, with a ripe imagination, with a power strengthened by knowledge of the world, and this is why great thinkers, great theologians, and great statesmen have gained from his writings a refreshment they could not find elsewhere.[1] I do not think there is one of the romances, unless it be *Castle Dangerous*, which is not likely to give you pleasure, for even *Count Robert of Paris*, written when mind and body were alike enfeebled, has chapters

[1] It is interesting to remember that in his last illness Mr. Gladstone re-read several of the Scotch novels which had delighted him in earlier years.

which only Scott could have produced.
The earlier novels of the series are generally
thought the greatest, but even in this respect
there is a variety of opinion.   The poets
William Morris and Dante Rossetti thought
St. Ronan's Well one of the best, and it has
been said—but if the tale be true, it is an exception to the rule—that when a number of
distinguished men wrote down separately the
name of their favourite Waverley novel, it
was found when the papers were compared
that each of them had given the palm to
St. Ronan's.   I think *Redgauntlet*, which
appeared in the same year, has more
admirers and deserves more.   Dear also to
many readers is *Anne of Geierstein*, although
it is far from being a general favourite.   In
Anne the great magician carries us into
Switzerland, where he had never been, and
I do not remember any descriptive passage
from Scott's pen more vivid and forcible
than Sigismund Biederman's narrative of the
battle of Granson, in which the Swiss con-
federates defeated the splendid army of the
proud Duke of Burgundy, who regarded
them as unruly mountain peasants, whose destruction would be a matter of small account.
This Sigismund, I must tell those of you
who do not know the story, was considered

the least promising of his family, slow in
understanding, if not mentally deficient,
but the brave fellow had a strong arm and
a warm heart, and sufficient sense to know
when he could most effectively help a friend.
You will find Sigismund's account of the
battle in the thirty-second chapter of the
novel.   I should like, did time allow, to
read the whole to you, for as Sigismund
warms to his story, you see all the rush
and circumstance of war, the glittering of
the spears, the eager attack of the cavalry,
the masterly tactics of the mountaineers, and
hear reverberated from the mountains the
thunder of the captains and the shouting ;
but listen to the conclusion of the story.
After describing some hand-to-hand fighting
on the crags, he goes on to tell of the
main battle in the plain :—

Lo you, we had scarce arrayed our ranks,
when we heard such a din and clash of instru-
ments, such a trample of their great horses, such a
shouting and crying of men, as if all the soldiers
and all the minstrels in France and Germany
were striving which should make the loudest
noise.   Then there was a huge cloud of dust
approaching us, and we began to see we must
do or die, for this was Charles and his whole

army come to support his vanguard. A blast from the mountain dispersed the dust, for they had halted to prepare for battle. Oh, good Arthur! you would have given ten years of life but to have seen the sight. There were thousands of horse, all in complete array, glancing against the sun, and hundreds of knights with crowns of gold and silver on their helmets, and thick masses of spears on foot, and cannon, as they call them. I did not know what things they were, which they drew on heavily with bullocks, and placed before their army, but I knew more of them before the morning was over. Well, we were ordered to draw up in a hollow square, as we are taught at exercise, and before we pushed forwards, we were commanded, as is the godly rule and guise of our warfare, to kneel down and pray to God, Our Lady, and the blessed saints; and we afterwards learned that Charles, in his arrogance, thought we asked for mercy. Ha! ha! ha! a proper jest. If my father once knelt to him, it was for the sake of Christian blood and godly peace; but on the field of battle, Arnold Biederman would not have knelt to him and his whole chivalry, though he had stood alone with his sons on that field. Well, but Charles, supposing we asked grace, was determined to show us that we had asked it at a graceless face, for he cried, " Fire my

cannon on the coward slaves; it is all the
mercy they have to expect from me!"—Bang—
bang—bang—off went the things I told you
of, like thunder and lightning, and some mischief
they did, but the less that we were kneeling ;
and the saints doubtless gave the huge balls a
hoist over the heads of those who were asking
grace from them, but from no mortal creatures.
So we had the signal to rise and rush on, and I
promise you there were no sluggards. Every
man felt ten men's strength.   My halberd is no
child's toy—if you have forgotten it, there it
is—and yet it trembled in my grasp as if
it had been a willow-wand to drive cows
with.   On we went, when suddenly the cannon
were silent, and the earth shook with another
and continued growl and battering, like thunder
under ground.   It was the men-at-arms rushing
to charge us.   But our leaders knew their trade,
and had seen such a sight before—It was, Halt,
halt—kneel down in the front—stoop in the
second rank—close shoulder to shoulder like
brethren, lean all spears forward, and receive
them like an iron wall!   On they rushed, and
there was a rending of lances that would have
served the Unterwalden old women with splinters
of firewood for a twelvemonth.   Down went
armed horse—down went accoutred knight—
down went banner and bannerman—down went

peaked boot and crowned helmet, and of those who fell not a man escaped with life. So they drew off in confusion, and were getting in order to charge again, when the noble Duke Ferrand and his horsemen dashed at them in their own way, and we moved onward to support him. Thus on we pressed, and the foot hardly waited for us, seeing their cavalry so handled. Then if you had seen the dust and heard the blows! the noise of a hundred thousand thrashers, the flight of the chaff which they drive about, would be but a type of it. On my'word, I almost thought it shame to dash about my halberd, the rout was so helplessly piteous. Hundreds were slain unresisting, and the whole army was in complete flight.

And here I want to say a word or two about Scott's prose style. In judging of it, we must remember the aim and method of the writer. There was very much of the improvisatore in the genius of Scott. Neither in verse nor prose does he linger daintily over words ; but, on the other hand, there is nothing artificial, nothing of the mannerist about him ; and when he has a great scene to describe, a scene which stimulates the imagination, his language is always adequate. Sometimes it is far otherwise, but if he is not a master of style, he is never mastered by it, as some authors of our own day have been. The simplicity that marked Sir Walter's character is seen also in his works.

The author of *Marmion* and of *Ivanhoe* never fails for want of vigour, and never loiters by the way when the plot requires that he should move over the ground swiftly. Where Scott does loiter is in the copious introductions to his novels which may be found tedious by young readers, and there is no reason why they should not be skipped for the present. They have an interest of their own which will be discovered later on.

Dean Stanley, in an address to students many years ago, spoke of "the profound reverence, the lofty sense of Christian honour, purity, and justice that breathe through every volume of the romances of Walter Scott." This is most true. True virtue and true religion are always reverently treated by him, and if he laughs at the eccentricities and quaint expressions of Puritan or Covenanter, he never despises a man, however fanatical he may be, whose faith is genuinely sincere. David Deans, in *The Heart of Midlothian*, for instance, is a

narrow-minded Cameronian who, when his
poor daughter Effie was accused of child-
murder, refused to have a lawyer to defend
her whose theological views were not what
he considered sound.   After declining one
advocate after another on the ground that
they were not faithful to the Cause, Davie,
when asked to try a lawyer named Mac-
kenzie, exclaims :—

   " If the life of the dear bairn that's under a
suffering dispensation, and Jeanie's, and my ain,
and a' mankind's, depended on my asking sic a
slave o' Satan to speak a word for me or them,
they should a' gae doun the water thegither for
Davie Deans !" . . . . " But, sir," continued Butler,
" we must use human means.   When you call in
a physician, you would not, I suppose, question
him on the nature of his religious principles ! "
" Wad I *no ?* " answered David—" but I wad,
though ; and if he didna satisfy me that he had
a right sense of the right hand and left hand
defections of the day, not a goutte of his physic
should gang through my father's son." . . . " This
is too rigid an interpretation of your duty,' sir.
The sun shines, and the rain descends, on the
just and unjust, and they are placed together in
life in circumstances which frequently render
intercourse between them indispensable, perhaps

that the evil may have an opportunity of being converted by the good, and perhaps, also, that the righteous might, among other trials, be subjected to that of occasional converse with the profane." "Ye're a silly callant, Reuben," answered Deans, "with your bits of argument. Can a man touch pitch and not be defiled? Or what think ye of the brave and worthy champions of the Covenant, that wadna sae muckle as hear a minister speak, be his gifts and graces as they would, that hadna witnessed against the enormities of the day? Nae lawyer shall ever speak for me and mine that hasna concurred in the testimony of the scattered, yet lovely remnant, which abode in the clifts of the rocks."

Yet in spite of the absurd intolerance that would have risked a daughter's life, Scott makes us respect Douce Davie, not of course for his prejudices, but for his fidelity to conscience. And David's eldest daughter Jeanie, a homely-looking, peasant girl, as faithful to her convictions as her father was, and with little to recommend her beyond nobility of character, is the heroine of the novel and one of the finest heroines in fiction. She will not say an untrue word to save her sister; but she who had hitherto rarely been beyond her father's cottage, will venture to go alone on foot from Edinburgh to London in order to appeal to Queen Caroline for the pardon of poor Effie. The difficulties and dangers she meets with on the road only serve to add to our respect for the faithful maiden, and when, through the Duke of Argyle, Jeanie gains access to the Queen, she wins her cause by a burst of natural eloquence quite in keeping with the simplicity of her nature.

I must explain to those of you who are unfamiliar with this novel, that Jeanie's story is associated with an historical event. Captain Porteous, a cruel man, having been sentenced to death in Edinburgh for murder, was reprieved at the last moment by the Government, and the indignant mob took the law into their own hands, broke open the Tolbooth prison, and hanged the captain on the spot where his crime had been committed. Her Majesty asks Jeanie if any friends of hers were engaged in the Porteous mob :—

" No, madam," answered Jeanie, happy that the question was so framed that she could, with a good conscience, answer it in the negative.

" But I suppose," continued the Queen, " if you

were possessed of such a secret, you would hold it a matter of conscience to keep it to yourself?"

" I would pray to be directed and guided what was the line of duty, madam," answered Jeanie.

"Yes, and take that which suited your own inclinations," replied her Majesty.

" If it like you, madam," said Jeanie, " I would hae gaen to the end of the earth to save the life of John Porteous, or any other unhappy man in his condition ; but I might lawfully doubt how far I am called upon to be the avenger of his blood, though it may become the civil magistrate to do so. He is dead and gane to his place, and they that have slain him must answer for their ain act. But my sister, my puir sister, Effie, still lives, though her days and hours are numbered ! She still lives, and a word of the King's mouth might restore her to a broken-hearted auld man, that never in his daily and nightly exercise, forgot to pray that his Majesty might be blessed with a long and a prosperous reign, and that his throne, and the throne of his posterity, might be established in righteousness. O madam, if ever ye kend what it was to sorrow for and with a sinning and a suffering creature, whose mind is sae tossed that she can be neither ca'd fit to live or die, have some compassion on our misery !—Save an honest house from dishonour, and an unhappy girl, not eighteen years of age, from an early and dreadful death! Alas! it is not when we sleep soft and wake merrily ourselves that we think on other people's sufferings. Our hearts are waxed light within us then, and we are for righting our ain wrangs and fighting our ain battles. But when the hour of trouble comes to the mind or to the body—and seldom may it visit your Leddyship—and when the hour of death comes, that comes to high and low—lang and late may it be yours!—Oh, my Leddy, then it isna what we hae dune for oursells, but what we hae dune for others, that we think on maist pleasantly. And the thoughts that ye hae intervened to spare the puir thing's life will be sweeter in that hour, come when it may, than if a word of your mouth could hang the haill Porteous mob at the tail of ae tow [the end of a rope].

Well may the Queen exclaim that this is eloquence, but it is eloquence in harmony with Jeanie's character, which is indeed drawn throughout with the hand of a great master. Scott has always an eye and heart for what is really noble in humanity, and this fine faculty enables him to discover the soul of beauty in men and women of the humblest order. There is a striking illustration of this in the trial scene of Fergus

Mac-Ivor in *Waverley*. Fergus is attainted of high treason, and so also is his faithful follower, Evan Maccombich. Evan is asked if he has anything to say for himself, and rising up, seemed anxious to speak. " But the confusion of the court and the perplexity arising from thinking in a language different from that in which he was accustomed to express himself kept him silent. There was a murmur of compassion among the spectators from the idea that the poor fellow intended to plead the influence of his superior as an excuse for his crime. The judge commanded silence and encouraged Evan to proceed :—

" I was only ganging to say, my Lord," said Evan, in what he meant to be an insinuating manner, "that if your excellent honour, and the honourable Court, would let Vich Ian Vohr go free just this once, and let him gae back to France, and no to trouble King George's government again, that ony six o' the very best of his clan will be willing to be justified in his stead ; and if you'll just let me gae down to Glennaquoich, I'll fetch them up to ye mysell, to head or hang, and you may begin wi' me the very first man." Notwithstanding the solemnity of the occasion, a sort of laugh was heard in the court

at the extraordinary nature of the proposal.
The Judge checked this indecency, and Evan,
looking sternly around, when the murmur abated,
" If the Saxon gentlemen are laughing," he said,
" because a poor man, such as me, thinks my life,
or the life of six of my degree, is worth that of
Vich Ian Vohr, it's like enough they may be
very right ; but if they laugh because they think
I would not keep my word, and come back to
redeem him, I can tell them they ken neither
the heart of a Hielandman, nor the honour of a
gentleman."

There are novelists who find all the food
for their fancy in the joys and troubles
of the poor. Scott's range was wider ; he
touches life at many points, and is as much
at home in a palace as in a cottage, in a
battlefield as in a law court, in depicting a
king like James I. or Louis XI., a soldier
of fortune like Sir Dugald Dalgetty, a
blind beggar like Willie Steenson, and an
innkeeper like Meg Dods. At the same
time, no poet or romance-writer has shown
a keener perception of the fine qualities so
often seen in lowly life, or has represented
them with greater sympathy and reverence. I will not occupy our time with
long quotations from volumes which, like

the *Waverley Novels*, are, or ought to be, in every library; and as a beautiful illustration of Sir Walter's genius in describing the affliction that places rich and poor upon a level, and gives dignity to both, I will ask you, while reading *The Antiquary*, to note in chapters xxxi. and xxxii. the fisherman Saunders Mucklebackit's grief at the loss of his son.

Sir Walter acknowledged, and justly, that he was a bad hand at depicting a hero. I do not think he has invented one who has much to recommend him beyond courage, fidelity, and good looks; and, with the exception of Diana Vernon, Jeanie Deans, Margaret Ramsay, and Rebecca the Jewess, the same may be said, perhaps, of his heroines. He is deficient also, and this is Scott's most prominent defect, in his love passages; but though weak in this respect, he is strong in delineating the other great passions which sway human nature; and when he gives full scope to his genius, and rises as far as prose permits to a poetical height, Scott is always great. He is a master, too, in the description of commonplace affairs and people. The talk of folk at inns, by the roadside, or in the village shop, of rustic lovers, of gipsies or fish-wives, of justices

of the peace, "dressed in a little brief
authority," and of people partially insane,
is given with a truth to Nature which only
Shakespeare has surpassed. Sir Walter
has a business-like capacity for details on
which he is sometimes fond of dwelling,
but while he has a firm foot on his mother
earth, the life he exhibits is glorified by a
poet's imagination.

My theme is so agreeable that I am
tempted to talk over it in too leisurely a
fashion. I should like, had time permitted,
to give some illustrations of Scott's racy
humour, of his profound pathos, often called
forth by the sorrows of the humblest people;
of his great tragic power which probably
reaches its height in *The Bride of Lammermoor*, and of the love with which he dwells
on the different aspects of Nature. It has
been said that of all the great names of
literature, none was so dear to Dean Stanley
as that of Walter Scott.

"They won't beat Sir Walter in a hurry!"
was the exclamation of Tennyson's friend
FitzGerald after reading *The Pirate.* Tennyson, too, as you will remember, wished it had
been his lot "to have heard him and seen
him and known"; and Hawthorne, the
American novelist, after saying how much

Scott had done for his happiness when young, added :—

I still cherish him in a warm place, and I do not know that I have any pleasanter anticipation as regards books than that of reading all the novels over again.

The wish was fulfilled, and Hawthorne read them aloud to his family. Those evenings with Scott must have left many a grateful memory, and if I advise you to spend some of your leisure hours in Sir Walter's company, it is in the hope and belief that you will be repaid with recollections equally pleasant in the days to come.

SIXTH TALK

WHEN the news came on the morning of October 6, 1892, that the "one clear call," to quote his own words, had been heard by Lord Tennyson, it was felt that England had lost her dearest son, and since the death of Wordsworth, her most gifted poet. In one sense the voice of Tennyson is the voice of England, for he was, as no other modern poet has been, the interpreter of his age. There is probably no moral or intellectual problem of our time with which he had not grappled, and this conflict, instead of destroying his belief, did but lead him to ask for more reverence and for a larger hope.

> Our little systems have their day ;
>   They have their day and cease to be :
>   They are but broken lights of thee,
> And thou, O Lord, art more than they,

was the poet's cry more than forty years
ago, and nearly forty years later, so truly
have the different periods of his life been
linked by faith and hope, he wrote the
little poem *Crossing the Bar*, which has
soothed dying ears, and will, we may be
sure, continue to soothe them. Listen to
the final stanzas :—

> Twilight and evening bell,
>   And after that the dark !
> And may there be no sadness of farewell,
>   When I embark ;
>
> For tho' from out our bourne of Time and Place
>   The flood may bear me far,
> I hope to see my Pilot face to face
>   When I have crost the bar.

And there was surely no more sadness
of farewell than Nature calls for when a
husband and father passes away. The
poet's death was in harmony with his life.
All that makes this world beautiful and
worthy had been lavished upon him, and the
gifts of Nature and Fortune had served
only to develop what was good and great.
Throughout Tennyson's writings there is no
dark page that he could have wished can-
celled when the end drew near, and with
his name all that is best and purest in the

literature of the Victorian age will be for ever associated. Like Milton, Lord Tennyson knew that a poet's life should be itself a poem, and consummate artist though he was, he never deemed it necessary for the purposes of his art to descend into the sewers. It was fitting that such a man should be buried in the great Abbey, where he lies near his noble friend Browning, and not far from the dust of the supreme poet of *The Faërie Queene*, than whom not even Tennyson has sung more sweetly, although he speaks to his contemporaries in language more familiar and significant. Near each other in death, far happier was Tennyson in life, and it is sad to think that Spenser's brief course of forty-six years ended in no common suffering and sorrow. His home in Ireland was attacked and burnt by Irish rebels, an infant child, it is said, perished in the flames, and the poet, who with his wife escaped to London, died, it is supposed, shortly afterwards in great poverty. The deepest sorrows are not those of which the world is able to take count, but the outward lot of Lord Tennyson has been one of the serenest and happiest ever granted to a man of genius. How much that is true and beautiful would the world have lost if he had died at forty-six like Spenser, or at fifty-two like Shakespeare; and how happy was it for him that the weight of eighty-three years was borne with bodily comfort and affected neither intellect nor heart. He was one of the few favoured ones

> who all the way
> To Heaven have a summer's day.

For most of us such unalloyed prosperity would probably be an evil and not a good, since man's choicest gifts are generally gained through sorrow. If this be true of all men, it is pre-eminently true of poets, who

> Learn in suffering what they teach in song.

Lord Tennyson, as you probably know, concentrated the energy of his life and intellect upon poetry. He felt that this great vocation was worthy of his highest efforts, and became a consummate master of the noblest of all arts. To know was as needful for him as to sing, and unlike his distinguished rival, Robert Browning, he has generally uttered his most beautiful thoughts in language as clear, as buoyant, and as musical as a mountain stream. Do not imagine that obscurity is always a sign of depth; it may be, and often is, an indication that a poet sees his subject from one side only. There is, indeed, a meaning in all poetry worthy of the name, invisible on the surface and hidden altogether from readers destitute of the poetic eye. A great poem yields something fresh upon every perusal, and its life-giving power is exhaustless, but it does not follow that the poet's primary meaning demands the aid of an interpreter. In breadth of sympathy and largeness of outlook Tennyson is the poet of his age, but he has avoided its literary defects, and has never forgotten that a poet's first duty is to sing. As a lyrical poet, considering the compass of his work, he has few rivals, and perhaps, in the delicate finish of his verse, no superior: "all the charm of all the Muses often flowering in a lonely word."

If you want to know or to recall the music of Tennyson's song, read and re-read *The Lotos-Eaters*, *The Brook*, the songs in *The Princess* and *Maud*, a lovely poem called *Early Spring*, published in one of his later volumes, and the familiar lyric (but not too familiar to be quoted) that is more than musically beautiful, since it embodies a pathetic truth which appeals to every one who has lived long enough to lose a friend :—

> Break, break, break,
>> On thy cold gray stones, O Sea !
> And I would that my tongue could utter
>> The thoughts that arise in me.
>
> O well for the fisherman's boy,
>> That he shouts with his sister at play !
> O well for the sailor lad,
>> That he sings in his boat on the bay !
>
> And the stately ships go on
>> To their haven under the hill ;
> But O for the touch of a vanish'd hand,
>> And the sound of a voice that is still !
>
> Break, break, break,
>> At the foot of thy crags, O Sea !
> But the tender grace of a day that is dead
>> Will never come back to me.

And here is another lyric of almost equal beauty :—

> Flow down, cold rivulet, to the sea,
>> Thy tribute wave deliver :
> No more by thee my steps shall be,
>> For ever and for ever.

Flow, softly flow, by lawn and lea,
  A rivulet then a river:
No where by thee my steps shall be,
  For ever and for ever.

But here will sigh thine alder tree,
  And here thine aspen shiver;
And here by thee will hum the bee,
  For ever and for ever.

A thousand suns will stream on thee,
  A thousand moons will quiver;
But not by thee my steps shall be,
  For ever and for ever.

Music is but one of many poetical gifts which Lord Tennyson can claim. No poet has given us such vivid and accurate representations of English scenery, or more lovely pictures of what is beautiful in English rural life. Read *The Gardener's Daughter*, *The Miller's Daughter*, and that charming poem, *The Talking Oak*, as illustrations of the poet's genius in this direction; and in narrative and idyllic verse the firm and delicate hand of a great master is visible in *Enoch Arden*, in *The Princess*, and above all, in *The Idylls of the King*, a poem which it has been rightly said shows more comprehensively than any other single work the range of Tennyson's power. Unlike his predecessor in the Laureateship he is also a humorist, and is strikingly original in his dialect poems, such as *The Grand-mother* and *The Northern Farmer*. More-over, the author of *The Two Voices*, and of *In Memoriam*, the most significant poem written in the last half-century, is, as I have said already, a deeply reflective poet, and, in the best sense of the word, Christian. It would be rash to pronounce confidently on the lasting power of any modern poem, but this at least may be said that, if *In Memoriam* as a whole should lose its hold on thoughtful readers, there are in it lines and stanzas which will be cherished as long as there are men and women who can appreciate lofty thoughts expressed with the perfection of poetic art. It is not, indeed, a poem for readers untried by the sorrows and conflicts of life, and you will take up *In Memoriam* with greater interest when the first freshness of youth is over. The versatility of Lord Tennyson in the choice and treatment of his sub-jects has done much towards making him the most popular of modern poets. Not Milton's blank verse is more distinctly his own than Tennyson's, and, as a lyric poet, he has tried many measures and excelled in all. The variety of his genius is remarkable. The author of the noble *Ode on the Death of the Duke of Wellington*—

> England's greatest son,
> He that gain'd a hundred fights,
> Nor ever lost an English gun ;

of that spirit-stirring ballad, *The Revenge*, and of *Rizpah*, the most powerfully tragic poem written in recent days, is also the author of *The May Queen* and of the simple lines, *In the Children's Hospital.* Dr. Johnson once advised a man to read whatever pleased him, advice which should not be accepted too literally, because in all productive reading strenuous effort must precede the pleasure which we owe to achievement ; but it is, I think, safe counsel to give a youthful reader on his first introduction to the works of a famous poet. He must be allured by the charms of meadow and woodland, before asking him to undertake the toil of a steep ascent. Read then, at first, what and where you please in Tennyson, and afterwards, if, as I always take for granted, you have an instinctive appreciation of what is beautiful in verse, you will discover much to delight you in what, for lack of a better term, may be called his poetical philosophy.

Of Tennyson it has been well said by his friend and brother-poet, Mr. Aubrey de Vere, that—

Since Shakespeare and since Wordsworth none hath
  sung
So well his country's greatness: none hath given
Reproof more fearless, or advice more sage,
None inlier taught how near to earth is Heaven.

Lord Tennyson had two brothers who possessed in their measure the gift in which he was pre-eminent. Frederick, the second son of the family, and Alfred's elder brother, who died in February 1898, lived much abroad, chiefly in Italy, and later on in Jersey. "Robert," Mrs. Browning writes, "is very fond of him, and so am I"; and of his poems she says that they are very melodious, but vague. "It's the smell of a rose rather than a rose—very sweet—notwithstanding." This is quite true; so sensitive was Frederick Tennyson to the music of verse, that it is perhaps the chief characteristic of his poetry which is lacking in strength. "Music," he said, "is the Queen of the Arts"; and much as he valued Robert Browning as a friend, he could not put up with what he calls "absolute horrors and unrhythmical composition," which is taking a very one-sided view of Browning's

art as a poet. Frederick Tennyson's poems
display all "the accomplishment of verse,"
without the freshness and strength that
give verse vitality. That at least is my
impression, but it may be a false one, for I
have never been able to read his poetry
with the attention it perhaps deserves. It
does not "find me," to use the significant
expression of another poet. Charles Tennyson, who, on succeeding to the estate of a
great-uncle, took the name of Turner, was
also an elder brother of the Poet-Laureate,
and *The Poems by Two Brothers*, published
in 1827, represent the youthful work of
both. Charles, who married Lady Tennyson's sister, lived the peaceful, happy life of
a country clergyman. His chief ambition
was to be good and to do good, and how
his brother loved him may be seen in the
stanzas written shortly after his death in
1879, in which he sees the present in the
light of "sixty years away" :—

> When all my griefs were shared with thee,
> And all my hopes were thine—
> As all thou wert was one with me,
> May all thou art be mine !

Charles Tennyson Turner's verse was
suggested by the simple incidents of daily

life : by the Nature that he loved, and the affections which he cherished. Unlike his brother, he chose the sonnet for the form in which to utter his song, and the sonnet, as I have said before, does not generally attract youthful readers. Some day you will read his volume, I hope, and delight in the exquisite pictures it contains of English scenery, and especially of child-life, a subject to which Charles Turner returns again and again and treats with a peculiar charm. One very characteristic poem called *Letty's Globe* shall be read to you, and then we must part from this true poet whom Cowper would have loved, and whose earliest work won the praise of Coleridge :—

When Letty had scarce pass'd her third glad year,
And her young, artless words began to flow,
One day we gave the child a coloured sphere
Of the wide earth, that she might mark and know,
By tint and outline all its sea and land.
She patted all the world; old empires peep'd
Between her baby fingers; her soft hand
Was welcome at all frontiers. How she leap'd
And laugh'd and prattled in her world-wide bliss;
But when we turn'd her sweet unlearned eye
On our own isle, she raised a joyous cry,
"Oh! yes, I see it, Letty's home is there!"
And while she hid all England with a kiss,
Bright over Europe fell her golden hair.

Of living poets and imaginative writers it is not my purpose to speak to you, but there are two famous poets who have passed away who demand a brief notice even in this slight survey.

Before, however, talking to you about them, let me remind you once more, as I am forcibly reminded myself, on glancing back on the subjects to which your attention has been called, that in these excursions in the Realms of Gold many of its loveliest regions, so far from being explored, have been barely skirted, while of others, not even the hastiest glimpse has been attained. The purpose of our journey indeed made this inevitable. My object, as you know, was to point out a few prominent features of the country, not to carry you through it, and yet I cannot but feel regret that so many spots which have been all my life dear to me have remained unvisited and even un-mentioned.

To drop the metaphor. It seems strange to me, for instance, to think that beyond the notice of his name, I have said nothing to you of Charles Lamb, whose essays and letters have a charm quite distinct, I think, from that which any other writer can claim. I do not say that *Elia* is greater or more delightful than some authors who have been mentioned ; but that for humour, for imagination, and for a tenderness which is infinitely attractive he stands apart from any of them. His place in our literature is one of the most enviable, for every reader who has felt the charm of his work loves the man.

" There are some reputations," Southey wrote on hearing of his death, " that will not *keep*, and must therefore be brought to market while they are fresh. But poor Lamb's is not of that kind ; his memory will retain its fragrance as long as the best spice that ever was expended upon one of the Pharaohs."

Some talk, too, I should like to have had about Christina Rossetti, best known to young readers as the author of the *Goblin Market*, whose perfection as a poetical artist is as remarkable as the freshness of her fancy and the depth of her feeling. To her I may apply the words of Wordsworth and say that

> You must love her ere to you
> She will seem worthy of your love.

Let me read to you one joyous lyric of hers before passing to " fresh fields " :—

My heart is like a singing bird
Whose nest is in a watered shoot;
My heart is like an apple-tree
Whose boughs are bent with thick-set fruit;
My heart is like a rainbow shell
That paddles in a halcyon sea;
My heart is gladder than all these
Because my love is come to me.

Raise me a dais of silk and down;
Hang it with vair and purple dyes,
Carve it in doves and pomegranates,
And peacocks with a hundred eyes;
Work it in gold and silver grapes,
In leaves and silver fleur-de-lys;
Because the birthday of my life
Is come, my love is come to me.

It is seldom that Christina Rossetti's verse is so jubilant. She learnt much and chiefly through suffering, and her songs are for the most part of the hopes and struggles and fears of the pilgrim, as, sometimes falling, and sometimes victorious, he fights his way to the better country. This century has produced a large amount of sacred verse, but surely none that is more likely to live than the heart-songs of Miss Rossetti.

One of the most copious poets of the day is William Morris, who died in 1896. His works have been published in ten volumes, and it is no great disparagement of his art to say that his exhaustive capacity for verse-making sometimes taxes the reader's patience too heavily.

The Earthly Paradise, his longest and finest poem, fills four goodly volumes; his *Life and Death of Jason* requires for the telling considerably more than 10,000 lines; another thick volume contains *The Story of Sigurd the Volsung*. *The Defence of Guenevere*, *Poems by the Way*, and *Love is Enough* are printed in two volumes, and the translations of the *Odyssey* and of the *Æneid* increase the bulk and add largely to the value of Morris's poetical works.

Now it will be seen at once that a poet who comes before the world with so vast a body of verse must have no insignificant merit in order to justify his pretensions. We are not so tolerant as our forefathers, who, when they wanted fiction, would wade through the stupendous romances of Mademoiselle de Scudery, and when their minds were bent on poetry, knew how to tolerate the wearisome epics of good Sir Richard Blackmore. The life of most readers nowadays can be sustained without a large proportion of poetical food, and it speaks well for the estimation in which Morris is held that his poems have passed through

several editions.   Such an honour has been
denied in their lifetime to some of the
greatest of modern poets, and it will be
interesting to ascertain how an author so
voluminous has won so large a reputation.

His merits lie, for the most part, upon
the surface.   This is the age of fiction, and
Mr. Morris in the art of story-telling in
verse is without any modern rival.   Then,
again, he is eminently lucid.   Like Macaulay
in prose, the reader is never for a moment
in doubt of the writer's meaning.   His
verse, which demands no intellectual effort,
glides on without a break, and resembles a
tranquil stream whose music lulls us as we
listen to it, and whose clear depth can be
readily seen and measured as our boat floats
upon its waters.   The calmness of such a
river is apt to become monotonous if we
sail on it too long, and sameness, unless
the reader is in a very tolerant mood, will
probably be felt, if he makes Morris his
companion for any lengthened period.   But
then the poet does not often ask us to stay
with him for long at a time.

The Earthly Paradise, like Chaucer's
Canterbury Tales, contains a variety of
stories linked together by a thread, which
is of the slightest texture, so that the reader,

being at liberty to take or to reject what he pleases, can escape the sense of weariness.

Chaucer, the first poet in our literature that deserves the name—the first poet that is to say who, however archaic his language may be, can be said to have written English, is "one of the world's three or four great story-tellers"; his love of Nature is sincere, though not displayed in the modern fashion, for he is content simply to enjoy and to describe, but the chief source of his inspiration is to be found in the lives of men and women.

His characters are all alive, and indeed so much alive that unfortunately the coarseness of the age is too often reflected in them. In a line, almost a word, a character is described. Chaucer's humour is unbounded, his pathos very simple and deep, and he wrote as few poets do nowadays, out of the abundance of a glad heart. Even when he aims at satire his method shows a kindly nature. It would be difficult to conceive of Chaucer scorning any one or doing an unkindly act, and he lives as a poet should do in an atmosphere of joy.

In his wealth of enjoyment he brings before the mind's eye many a gorgeous spectacle dazzling in colour. We hear the bray of the trumpet, the clashing of steel, the tramp of horses; or we listen to the songs of fair ladies, to the confessions of faithful lovers, to the light laughter of rustics. At one time Chaucer's world is homely and savours of the soil, at another he delights in portraying the splendour of tournaments and the revelry of courts. And all that he writes is apparently produced without effort. We are brought so near to the poet that it is as if we were hearing the story from his lips.

Although Mr. Morris calls Chaucer his "sweet-souled Master," there is little beyond an occasional quaint simplicity of phrase that recalls him to the mind. Of humour Mr. Morris has none, neither has he the power of drawing living men and women, and we miss that dew of the morning that gives freshness to the old poet's pages. His characters do not make the story, but serve as accessories — indispensable accessories — to the poet's narratives of adventure and descriptions of scenery. These remarks are true generally, and apply as much to *The Earthly Paradise* as to the *Jason*, but a poet who has written so much will doubtless occasionally contradict the verdict of his critic.

The argument of *The Earthly Paradise* is singularly adapted to Mr. Morris's peculiar genius. Certain gentlemen and mariners, hearing the report of a blessed country in the west where flowers never fade and men never grow old, sail across the sea to find it. They meet, as one might expect they would, with trouble upon trouble, and instead of gaining the life they sought, barely escape at last from the "ocean's weltering misery." And the sorrow was all the deeper because they believed at one time they had found the happy home they were seeking :—

> All hearts were melted and with happy tears,
> Born of the death of all our doubts and fears,
> Yea, with loud weeping, each did each embrace
> For joy that we had gained the glorious place.
> Then must the minstrels sing, then must they play
> Some joyous strain to welcome in the day,
> But for hot tears could see nor bow nor string,
> Nor for the rising sobs make shift to sing ;
> Yea, some of us in that first ecstasy
> For joy of 'scaping death went near to die.

At last, after many years, "with all hopes fallen away," the wanderers come to a quiet land where the elders of the town receive them kindly, and propose to hold two solemn feasts monthly at which they may relate tales of the past.

This plan affords the amplest scope to Mr. Morris's craft as a story-teller. Not only is he free to take what classical or mediæval legends he pleases, but his knowledge of Scandinavian literature is also used to good purpose. The author's distinguished merits may be seen in this elaborate work, and it will be unnecessary to go beyond it to discover the deficiencies which prohibit us from giving him a foremost place among the poets of the last half-century. Happily Morris understood the limitations of his genius. He rarely attempts to do what he cannot do well, and while never rising to a lofty height on the wings of poetry, never sinks to a low level. He is without what I may call spiritual ardour, without the vivid imagination that sends the blood bounding; the reader is seldom thrilled by his loveliest rhymes, but his perfect mastery of English and the ease with which he tells a story are merits that will, perhaps, always secure to him a ready audience.

Let the reader open *The Earthly Paradise* or the *Jason* where he pleases, and he will find something to attract him. To enjoy a tale it should be read throughout, but it is not impossible to give some brief specimens of the poet's art as a verseman.

Of certain aspects of Nature Mr. Morris is a faithful chronicler, as every country lover will acknowledge. In *The Earthly Paradise* two stories are told monthly, and in the preludes to these stories the aspects of the months are sometimes happily described.

In June the old men sail up a stream to a feasting-place under the shade of lime trees.

> Most lovely was the time
> Even amidst the days of that fair clime,
> And still the wanderers thought about their lives,
> And that desire that rippling water gives
> To youthful hearts to wander anywhere.

On another cloudless June day :—

> These folk amid the trellised roses lay,
> And careless for a little while at least,
> Crowned with the mingled blossoms held their feast:
> Nor did the garden lack for younger folk,
> Who cared no more for burning summer's yoke
> Than the sweet breezes of the April-tide ;
> But through the thick trees wandered far and wide
> From sun to shade, and shade to sun again,
> Until they deemed the elders would be fain
> To hear the tale, and shadows longer grew :
> Then round about the grave old men they drew,
> Both youths and maidens ; and beneath their feet
> The grass seemed greener, and the flowers more
>   sweet
> Unto the elders, as they stood around.

And now take a lovely July picture of repose :—

> The earth no longer laboured ; shaded lay
> The sweet-breathed kine, across the sunny vale,
> From hill to hill, the wandering rook did sail,
> Lazily croaking, midst his dreams of spring,
> Nor more awake the pink-foot dove did cling
> Unto the beech-bough, murmuring now and then.
> All rested but the restless sons of men
> And the great sun that wrought this happiness,
> And all the vale with fruitful hopes did bless.

Scenes such as these, always faithful to Nature and always beautiful, abound in Morris's verse. The poet carries his readers into many countries, but his landscapes are generally English.

Vigorous action he fails to describe, but in pictures of quiet life and in such as admit of bright colour and graceful form, his hand is firm and his success often great.

Another descriptive scene may be taken from *The Man born to be King* :—

> So long he rode he drew anigh
> A mill upon the river's brim,
> That seemed a goodly place to him,
> For o'er the oily smooth millhead
> There hung the apples growing red,

And many an ancient apple-tree
Within the orchard could he see,
While the smooth mill walls white and black
Shook to the great wheel's measured clack,
And grumble of the gear within;
While o'er the roof that dulled that din
The doves sat crooning half the day,
And round the half-cut stack of hay
The sparrows fluttered twittering.

In the judgment of some critics Morris
has won a high reputation for his ballads.
The modern ballad, written in the old style
and suggested by old customs and supersti-
tions, is, I think, very seldom a success. The
simplest form of poetry is hardly fitted to
inspire nineteenth-century poets, and there
is generally a literary tone in these productions which mars their simplicity. The
ballad, as I have already said, fascinated
Scott, and his love for it excited an enthusiasm which led to some of his finest
earlier efforts; but his fire has not descended,
and the remarkable ballads written by such
poets as Rossetti, Mr. Swinburne, Mr.
Meredith, and William Morris strike one
as splendid literary productions rather than
inspired poems.

Morris's verse would be more delightful
if the poet's outlook were less sad, but a
mournful fatalism pervades the whole. The

shadow of Death broods over it, of Death that has no life beyond. Every lovely picture, every passionate yearning, all the sweetness of love, all the wisdom born of sorrow, whatever stimulates energy or incites to self-sacrifice, becomes in this poet's verse of the earth earthy, and lasts only until "the long long day of the darkness" brings us "to the end, and all is done."

This hopeless and heartless creed is expressed so constantly that it grows monotonous. The Egyptians, we may suppose, did not lose their appetite for the good things provided at a feast on account of the skeleton present, and Mr. Morris's readers may perhaps become accustomed to the sad refrain that follows every scene of gladness in his verse. The pitiful philosophy that counsels us to "rejoice lest pleasureless we die," is one that must of itself suffice to take the nobility from a poet's work, and as a teacher—for incidentally, although not directly, all true poets are teachers—Mr. Morris has nothing better to give. It would be easy for me to show to you the truth of this statement by quoting many passages from *The Earthly Paradise* and from *The Death of Jason*, but a few will suffice.

When sixty years are gone at most
Then will all pleasure and all pain be lost.

.   .   .   .   .   .

So let me now be merry with the best,

exclaims Jason.   And the wanderers, who,
having vainly sought an earthly Paradise,
found instead that their wasted life ended
"where all things end in death at last," are
still eager to gain some pleasure out of the
dregs of life; for—

Since a little life at least was left,
They were not yet of every joy bereft,

therefore—and I quote now some beautiful
lines from another part of the poem—

Therefore their latter journey to the grave
Was like those days of later autumn-tide,
When he who in some town may chance to bide
Opens the window for the balmy air,
And seeing the golden hazy sky so fair,
And from some city garden hearing still
The wheeling rooks the air with music fill,
Sweet hopeful music, thinketh, Is this spring,
Surely the year can scarce be perishing?
But then he leaves the clamour of the town
And sees the withered scanty leaves fall down,
The half-ploughed field, the flowerless garden-plot,
The dark full stream by summer long forgot,
The tangled hedges where, relaxed and dead,
The twining plants their withered berries shed,

And feels therewith the treachery of the sun,
And knows the pleasant time is well-nigh done.
On such St. Luke's short summer lived these men,
Nearing the goal of threescore years and ten.

At last the apathy of old age lulled to rest the hearts of the wanderers, and it sufficed that

They still might watch the changing world go by,
Content to live, content at last to die.
Alas ! if they had reached content at last,
It was perforce when all their strength was past ;
And after loss of many days once bright
With foolish hopes of unattained delight.

Their life had been a failure, and this they know full well :—

Lo !
A long life gone and nothing more they know—
Why they should live to have desire and foil,
And toil that overcome brings yet more toil
Than that day of their vanished youth, when first
They saw Death clear, and deemed all life accurst
By that cold overshadowing threat—the End.

Kiss me, love ! for who knoweth
What thing cometh after death ?

is the burden of a song in *Ogier the Dane.*
In *The Doom of King Acrisius,* the picture of the two lovers, Perseus and Andromeda, is a beautiful one, which it is a pleasure to read to you.

Then on a rock smoothed by the washing sea
They sat, and eyed each other lovingly.
And few words at the first the maiden said,
So wrapped she was in all the goodlihead
Of her new life made doubly happy now:
For her alone the sea-breeze seemed to blow,
For her in music did the white surf fall,
For her alone the wheeling birds did call
Over the shallows, and the sky for her
Was set with white clouds, far away and clear;
E'en as her love, this strong and lovely one
Who held her hand, was but for her alone.

"O love, to think that love can pass away," and that the day shall come when this shall be forgotten, is the sad thought of Andromeda amidst her joy; and Perseus in reply says if she needs must think of the dull night that is creeping on, then for that thought let her hold closer to her bliss.

If the remark be made that in this instance such thoughts and fears are in harmony with the characters, the answer is that in the poet's verses all the characters, whether Christian or Pagan, live and move for the purpose of getting what pleasures they can out of life before the inevitable hour leaves them stranded in the darkness.

William Morris has styled himself a dreamer of dreams, and to enjoy his poetry the reader must dream also. It carries us into a world of imagery and of poetic shapes, which are entirely distinct from the realities of life. The men and women, like the gods and goddesses of mythology which play their parts in these poems, float before us like shadows. We must not, however, complain that a poet does not give us what, by his own admission, he is incapable of giving, and it is not slight praise to say that his verse is a model of good English.

And now I will turn to a poet as popular as William Morris but of a different order. Coventry Patmore, who died in 1897, had two styles. He is the poet of home life, but his genius carried him also into a region in which the youthful reader will find the air oppressive. In his *Unknown Eros*, Patmore sang for the fit audience that can listen to a poet when, like the skylark, he has left the clear blue of heaven and is lost in a partial mist. Some of his odes are indeed steeped in mysticism, much of which is a reproduction of the symbolism in vogue in mediæval days. It would seem that he rejoiced in being obscure, for he observes in one of his essays, "that neither in ancient nor in modern times has there been a poet worthy of that sacred name who would not have been horrified had he fancied that the full meaning of some of his sayings could be discerned by more than ten in ten thousand of his readers." This is, I venture to think, an extreme exaggeration of the unquestionable truth that in all fine poetry there is, as I have already said, a deeper meaning than lies upon the surface, deeper, perhaps, than the poet himself suspects, but it is possible even for a poet to mistake obscurity and eccentricity for depth : possible that the seer, by gazing too long on the far distance, misses the loveliness lying at his feet.

Love, which has been the theme of all poets from the days of Petrarch to our own, is the subject from which in his earlier years Coventry Patmore derived his inspiration and gained his popularity. Other poets may have treated it with more passion, and with an art more exquisite, but in the purity and spiritual elevation which breathe through all that Patmore has written he has been surpassed by none. In singing of the glow and ardour of youth, of its hopes and aspirations, of all that gives dignity to manhood, and a winning charm and grace to woman, this poet is Lord Tennyson's laureate successor. *The Angel in the House, The Victories of Love*, and *Tamerton Church-Tower*, although far from faultless poems, and with unfortunate traces of what is known as "namby-pamby," are full of beautiful thoughts, and of an observation of Nature which betrays no common love.

Long quotations will be unnecessary, but it may not be amiss to give a few passages to illustrate the charm, and also the weakness, of the poet's work. The faults in these poems are due apparently to an unsuccessful endeavour to be simple, and in effect Patmore reminds the reader of some of the baldest passages of Crabbe, and even of the inimitable parody of Wordsworth which lives in *Rejected Addresses.* Such verses as the following mock simplicity in attempting to magnify the commonplace :—

> While thus I grieved and kissed her glove
>   My man brought in her note to say,
> Papa had bid her send his love,
>   And would I dine with them next day.

Again :—

> Good Mrs. Fife
> To my, "The Dean is he at home?"
> Said, "No, sir: but Miss Honor is."
> And straight not asking if I'd come,
> Announced me, "Mr. Felix, Miss,"
> To Mildred in the Study.   There
> We talked, she working.   We agreed
> The day was fine ; the Fancy Fair
> Successful ; "Did I ever read

De Genlis ? "   " Never."   " Do ! "   She heard
I was "engaged."   "To whom ? "   " Miss Fry.
Was it the fact ? "   " No ! "   "On my word !
What scandal people talked ! "

A beautiful passage taken from a lyric in
the second volume is marred, as you will see,
in one line by this affected homeliness.   A
lover is driven by a sudden storm to take
refuge under a cottage porch.

A voice so sweet that even her voice,
  I thought, could scarcely be more sweet,
As thus I stayed against my choice,
  Did mine attracted hearing greet;
And presently I turned my head
  Where the kind music seemed to be,
And where to an old blind man she read
  The words that teach the blind to see.
She did not mark me : swift I went,
  Thro' the fierce shower's whistle and smoke,
To her home, and thence her woman sent
  Back with umbrella, shoes and cloak.
The storm soon passed; the sun's quick glare
  Lay quenched in vapour fleecy, fray'd;
And all the moist delicious air
  Was filled with shine that cast no shade;
And when she came, forth the sun gleam'd,
  And clashed the trembling Minster chimes;
And the breath with which she thank'd me seem'd
  Brought thither from the blossomed limes.

No happier change was ever made than
when the early poets of this century, heralded

by Burns and Cowper, escaped from the conventional diction of the last.   The reaction, however, was too violent.   The poet, by the very nature of his gift, as indeed Patmore admits in one of his essays, must find the common language of daily life inadequate to express his passion.   No one proved this more strikingly than Wordsworth himself, when he had his "singing robes" on ; but when his inspiration failed him he could write—

> I've measured it from side to side,
> 'Tis three feet long and two feet wide—

just as Patmore could write—

> My dearest Niece, I'm charmed to hear
> The scenery's fine at Windermere—

neither of these poets being saved from such prosaic twaddle by a sense of humour.

It has been said in defence of *The Angel of the House* that its most familiar lines have a hidden meaning, but this is an assertion that might be made as readily with regard to *Little Jack Horner*, since in neither case can the contrary be proved.

Patmore is not an affluent poet, for two small volumes hold all the verse which he has not deliberately rejected.   In the narrative poems I believe that he chose an easy, familiar style, thinking it most in harmony with his themes. At the same time these poems contain many passages as terse in thought as they are graceful in expression. Here, for instance, are eight lines, headed *Prospective Faith* :—

> They safely walk in darkest ways
>> Whose youth is lighted from above,
> Where, through the senses' silvery haze,
>> Dawns the veiled moon of nuptial love.
> Who is the happy husband ? He
>> Who scanning his unwedded life,
> Thanks Heaven with a conscience free,
>> 'Twas faithful to his future wife.

And here, in four lines, a simple truth is conveyed in the most appropriate words :—

> That nothing here may want its praise,
> Know, she who in her dress reveals
> A fine and modest taste, displays
> More loveliness than she conceals.

Again, what can be more epigrammatic than the following ?—

> The bliss which woman's charms bespeak,
> I've sought in many, found in none !
> In many 'tis in vain you seek
> What only can be found in one.

Touchstone in *As You Like It* introduces Audrey to the Duke as "a poor virgin, sir,

an ill-favoured thing, sir, but mine own."
The slightest hint suffices for a poet, and
Touchstone's words may have suggested
these lines to Patmore :—

> "Thy tears o'erprize thy loss !   Thy wife,
>   In what was she particular ?
> Others of comely face and life,
>   Others as chaste and warm there are, ·
> And when they speak they seem to sing ;
>   Beyond her sex she was not wise ;
> And there is no more common thing
>   Than kindness in a woman's eyes ;
> Then wherefore weep so long and fast,
>   Why so exceedingly repine ?
> Say how has thy beloved surpass'd
>   So much all others ? "   "She was mine."

The inclination to quote dainty passages
from this poet's verse grows as one turns
over the pages. Wordsworth in his great
ode writes of the glad hearts that do the
work of duty without knowing it, and
Patmore strikes a similar note when he
writes of

> Souls found here and there,
>   Oases in our waste of sin,
> Where everything is well and fair
>   And Heaven remits its discipline.
> Whose sweet subdual of the world
>   The worldling scarce can recognise,
> And ridicule against it hurled
>   Drops with a broken sting and dies.

·   ·   ·   ·   ·

Who should their own life plaudits bring,
  Are simply vexed at heart that such
An easy and delightful thing
  Should move the minds of men so much.
They live by law, not like the fool,
  But like the bard, who freely sings,
In strictest bonds of rhyme and rule,
  And finds in them not bonds but wings.
Postponing still their private ease
  To courtly custom, appetite,
Subjected to observances,
  To banquet goes with full delight.
Nay, continence and gratitude
  So cleanse their lives from earth's alloy,
They taste in Nature's common food
  Nothing but spiritual joy.
They shine like Moses in the face,
  And teach our hearts without the rod,
That God's grace is the only grace,
  And all grace is the grace of God.

Among the poet's highly elaborate odes there is one so simple and so beautiful that it appeals to every heart, and is, probably on that account, familiar; yet, at the risk of repeating what you may know already, I must quote *The Toys*, both for its own merit and because it is peculiarly significant of the poet.

My little Son who looked from thoughtful eyes
And moved and spoke in quiet grown-up wise,
Having my law the seventh time disobeyed,

I struck him and dismissed
With hard words and unkissed,
His Mother who was patient being dead.
Then, fearing lest his grief should hinder sleep,
I visited his bed
But found him slumbering deep,
With darkened eyelids, and their lashes yet
From his late sobbing wet.
And I, with moan,
Kissing away his tears, left others of my own ;
For, on a table drawn beside his head,
He had put, within his reach,
A box of counters and a red-veined stone,
A piece of glass abraded by the beach
And six or seven shells,
A bottle with blue bells,
And two French copper coins, ranged there with
     careful art,
To comfort his sad heart.
So when that night I prayed
To God, I wept and said :
Ah when at last we lie with tranced breath,
Not vexing Thee in death,
And Thou rememberest of what toys
We made our joys,
How weakly understood
Thy great commanded good,
Then, fatherly not less
Than I whom Thou hast moulded from the clay,
Thou'lt leave Thy wrath and say
I will be sorry for their childishness.

I gave you a joyous love lyric of Miss
Rossetti's ; and now you shall hear how

Coventry Patmore treats the same theme. There is a delicious music and buoyant spirit in these lovely lines which ought to secure them a place in every selection of English verse :—

> Bright thro' the valley gallops the brooklet ;
> Over the welkin travels the cloud ;
> Touched by the zephyr dances the harebell ;
> Cuckoo sits somewhere, singing so loud ;
> Two little children, seeing and hearing,
> Hand in hand wander, shout, laugh, and sing ;
> Lo, in their bosoms, wild with the marvel,
> Love like the crocus is come ere the Spring.
> Young men and women, noble and tender,
> Yearn for each other, faith truly plight,
> Promise to cherish, comfort and honour :
> Vow that makes duty one with delight.
> Oh, but the glory found in no story,
> Radiance of Eden unquenched by the Fall :
> Few may remember, none may reveal it,
> This the first first-love, the first-love of all !

How much of Patmore's verse will outlive the stress of time it is not possible to say. Of this, at least, we may be certain, that the poet did not mistake his calling, and the memorable words which introduce the reprint of his *Poetical Works* show how high his aim had been and with what expectation and noble ardour he pursued it. "I have written little," he says, "but it is all my best : I have never spoken when I had nothing to say, nor spared time or labour to make my words true. I have respected posterity ; and should there be a posterity which cares for letters, I dare to hope that it will respect me."[1]

And now, before bidding farewell to the men

> Who on earth have made us heirs
> Of truth and pure delight by heavenly lays,

let me remind you that, although what I have said may be unworthy of the subject, all that is enchanting in music, and sweet or ennobling in thought, may be found in the poets of whom I have spoken. I can but talk, they can sing ; and if you have an ear to listen, you will gain a pleasure that does not fall away as you grow older, but will add a fuller and deeper joy to life as the years move on.

Once more let me urge you not to be satisfied with such knowledge of our poetical literature as can be gained from reading about it. All the talk and all the reading are worse than useless, unless you resolve to study the great works which the poets have left us,

[1] A considerable portion of the Talk about Morris and Patmore is, with the editor's kind permission, reprinted from the *Leisure Hour.*

unless you come to know these works not as school exercises, but as living creations. I am not asking you to gain this knowledge hurriedly or by wearisome efforts, but I do ask you not to rest content with the pleasant amusement of turning over poetical selections, or with reading criticisms, but thoroughly to study some great master like Spenser or Milton ; and while doing this you need not refrain from making many a pleasant ramble in what may be called the bypaths of poetry where the ground is covered with wild-flowers, and "beauty born of murmuring sound" fills the heart with gladness.

Bishop Butler, in his noble treatise, *The Analogy of Religion*, has called the imagination a "forward delusive faculty," and his book stands almost alone among English works of the highest order in the entire lack of that faculty. For, as I have insisted in these "Talks," imagination is the source of almost all that is highest in literature. Alone, indeed, or when simply allied to fancy, it may prove delusive, but when tempered with knowledge, with judgment, with breadth of thought, with human sympathy, and with the homely wisdom known as common sense, it becomes a gift of inestimable value.

236 The Realms of Gold

As you grow familiar with the landmarks
of literary history you will find, as I have
been at some pains to show you, that
not of verse alone, but also of prose,
imagination is one of the most distinct
and attractive features. If it forms the
life-blood of poetry, it dignifies the pages
of historians and illuminates the weighty
discourses of philosophers and divines.
Authors who do not possess this gift will be
read for their information and research, but
they have seldom any commanding influence.
The food they give us may help, in some
degree, to support the intellectual life, but
it neither invigorates nor inspires. Do not
suppose that there is any antagonism
between imagination and truth; on the
contrary, it is through the help of it that
we are best able to see into the life of things
and to estimate their value.

What Wordsworth calls "onward-looking
thoughts" are the thoughts inspired by
imagination which incites us to look "on
and always on." People who pride themselves on being matter-of-fact, regard imagination as something unreal and unwhole-
some. They will tell you that it unfits a
man for the practical duties of life, and
they will point, as they readily may, to

dreamy enthusiasts who have preferred living in the clouds to keeping a firm footing on their mother earth. My answer is, that if these impracticable beings were led astray by imagination, they abused a good gift which, to those who use it wisely, is a constant source of exhilaration and strength. In the poet it is a creative power enabling him, as Shakespeare says, to " body forth the forms of things unseen " ; for most of us it is no small boon if, by its help, we are able to see and to appreciate the shapes which the imaginative author has embodied in verse or prose.

To assist you a little in doing this has been the chief purpose of these " Talks." All I can hope to accomplish by them is to awaken a love of literature which, up to the present hour, may have been dormant, to show you in a slight degree what a glorious Realm lies open for you to enter, and to direct your first steps upon a road along which you may wander for a lifetime without exhausting its variety and beauty.

Printed by R. & R. CLARK, LIMITED, Edinburgh

www.ingramcontent.com/pod-product-compliance
Lightning Source LLC
Chambersburg PA
CBHW020109030726
47498CB00006B/2026